"What do you want?"

The question hung between them. Nate raised the champagne bottle to his mouth, tipping it back for a long swallow, before turning and pinning her to her spot with the full intensity of his gaze. "You. I want you, Payton. I need you to pretend we're involved. That we've been involved for the last month, actually."

Nate watched as Payton's face blanched and then went to beet-red. She sputtered at length before she finally nailed that single-word demand for clarification. *"What?"*

Well, he hadn't expected her to simply agree and climb into his lap.

And, man, as much as he liked the hot flush across her skin, he definitely didn't need to think of Payton's lush curves and petite frame curling into the seat of his thighs. Not a good idea at all. Never had been.

How was it he managed multibillion-dollar deals without batting an eye, but he couldn't spit out a simple illicit proposal with any clarity or finesse at all?

He let loose a frustrated growl. "Here's the deal. The press is onto me. Digging into something I don't want dug up. I need a distraction. Something juicy they can sink their teeth into. And I need a friend—someone I can trust— to help me pull it off. You're perfect. You're well-known, respected, and everyone will believe you wouldn't want a relationship with me publicized."

MIRA LYN KELLY grew up in the Chicago area and earned her degree in fine arts from Loyola University. She met the love of her life while studying abroad in Rome, Italy, only to discover he'd been living right around the corner from her for the previous two years. Having spent her twenties working and playing in the Windy City, she's now settled with her husband in rural Minnesota where their four beautiful children provide an excess of action, adventure and entertainment.

With writing as her passion, and inspiration striking at the most unpredictable times, Mira can always be found with a notebook at the ready. (More than once she's been caught by the neighbors, covered in grass clippings, scribbling away atop the compost container!)

When she isn't reading, writing or running to keep up with the kids, she loves watching movies, blabbing with the girls and cooking with her husband and friends. Check out her website at www.miralynkelly.com for the latest dish!

FRONT PAGE AFFAIR
MIRA LYN KELLY

~ ONE NIGHT AT A WEDDING ~

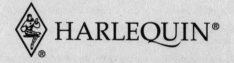

HARLEQUIN®

TORONTO • NEW YORK • LONDON
AMSTERDAM • PARIS • SYDNEY • HAMBURG
STOCKHOLM • ATHENS • TOKYO • MILAN • MADRID
PRAGUE • WARSAW • BUDAPEST • AUCKLAND

Recycling programs
for this product may
not exist in your area.

ISBN-13: 978-0-373-52800-4

FRONT PAGE AFFAIR

Previously published in the U.K. under the title
TABLOID AFFAIR, SECRETLY PREGNANT!

First North American Publication 2011

FRONT PAGE AFFAIR

To Mom and John, with countless thanks for showing me *true love* and *happily ever after* aren't just for stories.

CHAPTER ONE

FLASHBULBS exploded. Shutters snapped like automatic fire around him as reporters from rags of all caliber called for attention, each voice clamoring to rise above the rest.

"Mr. Evans!"

"One more over here!"

Beneath the awning of the exclusive Chicago hotel, Nate Evans offered up a stock smile, responded to a few light questions with a handful of ambiguous words and waited for the question he knew would come.

It didn't take long.

"Mr. Evans! Care to explain your sudden absence from the social circuit these past months?"

The question shot through the early autumn evening, silencing all others with its gathering strength while narrowing the focus on him like an interrogator's spotlight.

They knew when they were onto something.

But he was ready for the assault. Invited it.

Feigning surprise at the inquiry, Nate paused in mock consideration before answering. "Guess I've been so caught up in business, I hadn't realized I'd gone off the map."

His answer wouldn't satisfy even the most limited curiosity. And more than that, it was a lie. He'd spent the last six months laying low. Flying under the radar to avoid notice while the nightmare of his life slowly, painfully, worked itself toward an unsatisfactory resolution. Six months out of the limelight, away from the cameras, only to find his absence conspicuous enough in itself to fuel new rumors and speculation as to the cause.

Who's the beauty behind this bachelor's broken heart?

The squelched headline had hit him like a sucker punch to the gut and he'd spent a fortune making it go away. Buying time. But if he didn't get a stranglehold on the situation, the trash hounds would dig and dig until they found the truth. And then they'd keep digging, making such a muck and mess that the dirt slung in their quest for ratings would reach anyone and everyone even remotely tied to his life.

His dad didn't need that.

Neither did Bella, the tiny baby who'd dragged a commitment from his jaded heart with a fist too small to wrap around his thumb. She was pure and precious and new. And though she didn't belong to him, he'd sworn to protect her from whatever hardships he could. And preventing a media circus from assailing her home and her mother—who wasn't in any shape to defend against it—was top on the list.

Which brought him to tonight. The first who's-who gala event available to spin the press off his scent.

He smiled his best cat-about-to-give-the-canary-a-go smile for the cameras. "Better find out if any of the ladies still remember me." And with that parting sound bite, he jogged the few steps through the grand entrance, looking for all the world as though he didn't want to miss a minute. As though he wouldn't rather be in his physician's office turning his head to the left to cough, than heading into the "society wedding of the season".

He needed a diversion—and the sooner the better. So this was it.

He'd dive headfirst into tonight's sea of swank and silk, in search of the biggest scandal. He'd reel in a beauty he could splash across the tabloid pages. Someone with enough hook she'd drag the press's interest out of the past and secure it in the now.

Someone who knew the score.

That was the touchy part, because, when it came to his dates, Nate didn't do soft. He didn't do love. And he didn't do forever. He made certain his women knew what they were getting into with him—and then he did them with enough attention and skill they didn't care there wasn't anything deep or lasting between them.

Scanning the throngs of social elite gathered within the gold-domed ballroom, he searched for a like-minded wave-maker. Except after barely five minutes, Nate realized he'd miscalculated—and in no small way. Finding a woman to flaunt was easy. There were at least a hundred willing candidates batting thick-fringed lashes at him. But with each toss of perfectly coiffed hair and every lingering glance, the apathy that had kept him so easily unattached these past six months turned to something darker.

More suffocating. Everywhere he looked, false claims and secret agendas lurked beneath the guise of enticement, and he found himself backing away rather than closing in.

And then he saw her.

Payton Liss, slinking through the crowd, using every evasive technique at her disposal to dodge the conciliatory hand pats, air kisses and general gossipy blood sport that occurred post nuptials—regardless of the social strata involved.

The good girl from his past. Brandt's little sister. Miss Off-Limits herself.

Payton didn't need his money. She wouldn't want his name. And she'd help him regardless of what went down with Brandt all those years ago because she habitually did the right thing.

Or make that, she *mostly* did the right thing.

The corner of his mouth quirked as, while he watched, she pilfered a dinner roll from the table closest to the kitchen access hall and slipped stealthily out the door.

Nate's feet were moving before his brain had even finished processing the plan.

Neck deep in a cloud of ill-fitting taffeta and tulle, Payton Liss pressed her shoulders into the wall behind her. Stretching across the floor of her hideout—a miraculously unlocked utility room, discovered purely by accident three weddings before—she braced a foot against the door and straight-legged with the determination of a second-string bridesmaid on the run.

"Not a chance, Nate. The women will sniff you out. Go find your own storage closet."

Between the gap of the door and frame, ice-blue eyes slid over her, bringing to both mind and body the heart-pounding effect that gaze once elicited. "You open this door, Payton, or I'm heading straight back into that reception—and I'm telling every schmuck I can find you're alone in here...crying." The last word he delivered with the smug satisfaction of a man who knew he'd already won.

Her breath caught as she stared in outraged indignation. "I am not crying!" Hiding, yes. Sulking, some. Crying, not a chance.

"It'll be like open season. Every guy intent on snaring himself a top-floor job in Liss Industries moving in for his white-knight moment. And the talk..."

Her stomach seized. It was the talk that had driven her into hiding in the first place.

The "Poor Payton" talk.

"...Such a good girl...so desperate for a wedding of her own...so disappointed when he left her...what her father had wanted, but what did he expect..."

She couldn't stand the sound of it anymore.

. They were all wrong. But even if she bellowed out the truth, no one would believe her. She'd done too good a job for too long of forcing herself into the mold of a quiet-souled, docile-minded lady who didn't exist. And for nothing. In the end, no amount of perfect behavior could save her father from the weak heart that had plagued him the last fifteen years of his life.

Pushing back the well of emotion that still rose at the thought of losing him the year before, she shook her head. Nothing could upset him now. No defiant choice or willful stand for independence. He was at peace and, though his death broke her heart, it also set her free.

But no matter the changes she made, no one could see past the illusion she'd perfected to the real woman trying to break free. Which was why this had to be the last society event. She needed a life. One she could live on her own terms.

To try and set the record straight before she escaped would leave her sounding *petty*—the perfect complement to pre-existing *pathetic*.

No, thank you—

The bored sigh directed her way snapped Payton back to the present. To Nate, quite literally sticking his head back into her life after walking out of it all those years ago. "Last chance, babe, or I talk. Lot of hopefuls out there tonight waiting for a shot."

He'd do it, too, the bastard, she thought, giving into the inexplicable smile that seemed to rise from the ashes of every memory she had of the man. Nearly every memory anyway.

Nate knew no limits when it came to getting what he wanted. And now—after a decade with little more than the most limited greetings passing between them, and only when absolutely necessary—he wanted to get into her hideout.

"Now, Payton."

With a reluctant sigh, and then a second, louder, more pointed version of the first, she gave up her hold on the door and scooted into a seated position against the wall where she'd arranged a pile of linens to pad the floor.

"Fine, come in. Just hurry up before someone sees you."

"Smart girl." He shouldered through the door, closing it with the sweep of one foot behind him. The swift, fluid move, executed with Nate's signature masculine economy of motion, took her back to the days of watching him tear across the soccer field. Fast and strong and skilled. Damp strands of sun-kissed gold whipping about his face as he drove toward a goal.

She hadn't been able to take her eyes off him.

Even now, attempting to pry her gaze from the man-sized version of the boy she'd wanted so badly, she only managed to skirt from one hard-planed, deep-chiseled element of his physique to the next.

It was no good.

He was more devastating in the looks he'd grown into than any man had a right to be. The waves atop his head were a few shades darker and a bit shorter, but remained utterly tempting in their unruly disarray. He was broader in the shoulders and chest, still athletically lean and exuded a power and confidence that dwarfed the world around him. Particularly in his tailor-made tux with a bottle of champagne hanging loosely from his fingers. The personification of careless elegance.

Intimidating in ways to which she was normally immune.

But then, this was Nate. It had been different with him from the start. He was everything she never let herself be.

Finally she asked, "What are you doing back here?"

His cool blue gaze locked with hers, and the corner of his mouth twisted upward to the slightest degree. "Looking for you."

Not in the imminent seduction way it sounded, she was certain. Nate didn't think of her like that and never would. She peered up from her spot on the floor, waiting for him to elaborate, but he glanced around the small room instead, taking in the shelves stocked with miscellaneous serving equipment, a rolling cart, table dressings. "Nice place you've got here. Built-in sound system and everything," he said with a gesture to indicate the strains of "Get Down Tonight" filtering through the walls.

"Thanks, it's coming together quite nicely, I think. A few more weeks and I'll be ready to entertain."

He cocked a brow at the makeshift seating she'd assembled. His gaze darkened. "Not expecting company now, are you?"

Heat splashed up her neck and cheeks as she realized what her little sanctuary might suggest to a world-class player like Nate. "No, no." She shook her head, her hands flapping as her explanation tumbled out. "Just settling in for the long haul. I shouldn't be seen leaving for at least another hour, but with all the talk I just couldn't stand to stay."

"I get it. They're like a pack of vultures out there." He gave her hip an indelicate nudge with the toe of his shoe. "Move it, I want in on the nest."

Inching over, she made room as he knelt down—the heavy muscles of his thighs flexing beneath the hug of his trousers—and settled against the wall beside her. Her heart-rate went up with the temperature in a room she'd been sure was cool only moments ago.

Arms balanced atop his bent knees, he held the champagne in one wide palm, brushing his thumb through the condensation accumulating on the heavy glass. "What I can't understand is why the hell you would come alone. And I'm praying it isn't because you were hoping to hook back up with that chump ex of yours, Clint."

Payton rolled her eyes. Too much to hope that Nate wouldn't have heard the gossip surrounding her breakup. Yet another reason necessitating her imminent escape from the social scene. "No. God, no. This is my worst nightmare. I'd planned to come down with something contagious and unexpected and not be able to attend at all. But a bridesmaid beat me to it and I got promoted up from guest. Lucky me."

Nate's mouth twisted down as he looked her over. "If you say so."

She laughed out a breath and then turned, falling back into the conversation that had always come so easily between them. "Well, what about you? It's a wedding…and you've scored a slot on the world's most eligible bachelors list three years in a row. You'd need a date on each arm to escape unscathed. But stag? I'm amazed you made it out of the ballroom without the single girls setting up a numbered queue to get served."

"Get served?" This time it was Nate who laughed, letting his head loll back against the wall behind him. "Payton, Payton." He caught her with a questioning glance. "What kind of talk is that from a good girl like you?"

She stared at him, her heart skipping a beat as his focus shifted to her mouth.

"And why am I the only one who gets to hear that lip of yours?"

She couldn't have him looking at her like that, particularly when he had no intention of following through. She could handle her attraction to him, she'd done it for over half her life. Managed it. Tamped it down and stuffed it away. First because it was futile, and then because it was misplaced. But now… The last thing she needed was Nate reminding her of what she couldn't have. Flirting when he'd never see her as more than Brandt's little sister. The *good girl*.

Enough. She needed to know what the man who walked out of her life with barely a word all those years ago wanted with her now, and then she needed to get him out of her space before she did something stupid. Such as catch a bit of that unruly hair between her fingers and test its softness against her lips. "What do you want?"

The question hung between them. Nate raised the bottle to his mouth, tipping it back for a long swallow, before turning and pinning her to her spot with the full intensity of his gaze. "You. I want you, Payton."

CHAPTER TWO

"I NEED you to pretend we're involved. That we've been involved for the last month, actually."

Nate watched as Payton blanched and then went to beet, sputtering at length before she finally nailed that single-word demand for clarification. *"What?"*

Well, he hadn't expected her to simply agree and climb into his lap.

And, man, as much as he liked the hot flush across her skin, he definitely didn't need to think of Payton's lush curves and petite frame curling into the seat of his thighs. Not a good idea at all. Never had been.

"Take it easy, princess. Have a sip." He offered the champagne, only to have it pushed back at him. With a shake of her head, a silky blonde spiral sprang free at her temple. The first ruffled feather.

She was staring at him now, those big brown eyes wide with disbelief. "You want me to pretend we're together?"

A nod. "But you hadn't wanted us to get caught."

Her face screwed up. "Excuse me?"

How was it he managed multibillion-dollar deals without batting an eye when he couldn't spit out a simple illicit proposal with any clarity or finesse at all?

Letting loose a frustrated growl, he pushed his fingers into his hair, giving it a good tug at the root. "Here's the deal. The press is on me. Digging into something I don't want dug up. I need a distraction. Something juicy they can sink their teeth into. And I need a friend—someone I can trust—to help me pull it off. You're perfect. You're well known, respected, and everyone will believe you wouldn't want a relationship with me publicized."

"Why not?" she asked, and the way her brow furrowed in genuine confusion had Nate wanting to laugh.

"You're Payton Liss. You want a respectable husband. A tidy family." He tipped the bottle again and downed another swallow before turning back to her. "A blue-blood name."

And everyone knew Nate wasn't about marriage. There'd been a time, back when he first hit the financial papers, that women lined up with "love" in their eyes and a prenup in their purse. Talk about a turnabout for the kid who couldn't get a commitment for the prom because he didn't have a trust fund. But he wasn't a man built for love and lasting. And he didn't get played. Soon enough, the women in line weren't looking for anything more than he was. A little company and a lot of sweaty sex. Sure, the occasional fortune hunter still got her silk panties in a twist over his refusal to tie the knot...but on the whole, there weren't a lot of misconceptions about what he had to offer the women he dated.

A good time. On his terms.

The soft brown of her eyes seemed to go hard beneath his stare, her body still, her voice cool. "If those are my priorities then why would I have an affair with you?"

"Because I'm the best kind of forbidden fun," he answered with a cocky smile promising it was true. "A bit of slumming after things didn't work out with Clint. A palate cleanser before the next blue blood gets in line."

"Slumming?" she asked, incredulous. "You could buy and sell my family three times over."

Sure he could...now.

"The name thing," he offered with a shrug. "Old money versus new."

Payton's lips parted, then firmed into a tight line. A pretty pink stained her cheeks as she moved to stand. "No one would believe something so ridiculous and insulting."

Nate caught her wrist, pulling her back down. "Everyone believes it." He gently chucked under her chin. "But even if it's not true…there's still Brandt."

Brandt. The only reason she might say no.

She huffed, irritated. "Yes, and I don't particularly want my brother's wrath coming down on me over you—not without a good reason."

"How about this. Go along with my plan because it'll give the talk about you a whole new flavor. No more pity over that idiot not marrying you. They'll be shocked…and *jealous*."

Payton's expression lightened as she focused on some distant spot beyond the snug walls of their utility closet before returning to him. "Confidence is a real problem for you, isn't it?"

"Hey, you're the one who suggested the numbered queue." But his humor faded as he searched her eyes. "I need this. I need the press to stop looking for what I've been up to the last six months. I need them to think they've already found the big secret. That it's you. People will read a million reasons into why we didn't want it public.… Hope that Clint would come around. The animosity between your brother and me. The fact that women who date me aren't doing it in search of a happily ever after. Let them guess."

Payton's gaze shifted restlessly around their small space.

This was supposed to be it. The last society affair. She was getting out of the papers and getting on with the life she'd been working toward. The life where she was judged on her merit rather than how successfully she wore a gown or what the press reported her priorities to be.

But Nate would never have come to her if his secret wasn't important.

And she had to admit some brazen bit of her psyche, too long neglected, reveled in the stir the name Payton Liss paired with Nate Evans would cause. Definitely talk of a different flavor.

Brandt would be livid. Though her inward snicker quickly turned to pause. Whatever had transpired between Brandt and Nate hadn't been washed away by the passage of time. After ten years, the mere mention of Nate Evans put her brother into a lather…and she still didn't fully understand why. As she didn't understand why Nate had closed himself off from her so abruptly. So absolutely.

Casting a sidelong glance at the tuxedo-clad villain himself, she realized this could very well be her chance to find out.

"What happened with Brandt? Why did you hurt him that way?"

Nate's jaw set, the muscle jumping once before he answered. "Maybe Brandt deserved to be hurt a little."

Her brother had done a lot of things over the years she couldn't condone. Couldn't understand. In the back of her mind, she'd always suspected—

"Maybe he deserved worse." The ice blue of Nate's gaze raked over her in one slow, telling sweep before it locked back at her eyes. "I could have done worse."

Her mouth opened, to gasp or deny, only nothing came of it but a slow leaking breath that might have been regret. She would have given Nate anything. Done anything he asked.

If he'd decided to use her as a means of payback or revenge or whatever motivated him back then, he would have found no resistance. Only the eager willingness of a girl desperate for him to see her as a woman. And the repercussions… "Brandt would have gone nuts."

Nate let out a bark of laugher. "Yeah, well, it wasn't concern for your brother that stopped me."

A tide of warmth washed through her and she stole a glimpse his way. Her hero, always and in the most unconventional ways. Only he'd walked away from her as if their friendship meant nothing. "Where've you been all this time?"

Her quietly posed question brought a pause, and the faint lines around his eyes lost their laughter. "The last six months I've spent mostly in Germany." He shifted in the nest, stretching out one long leg before them. "Babysitting a new venture that didn't take off the way I'd anticipated."

It wasn't what she'd meant. She'd been thinking more of where he'd been for the past ten years. They'd been close. They'd been friends. And then one day, he just wasn't. Except now he was back. Asking her to be the friend he needed to help him.

"Do you want to tell me what this is all about?"

Nate ran a wide palm over the heavy line of his jaw. "Honestly, I'd like to get out of your little home-away-from-home here."

Pushing to his feet, he dug into his pocket for a handful of bills he then tucked under the champagne bottle left atop the rolling cart. "What do you say?" Catching her hand, he pulled her up with him. "Strength in numbers, right? We head back into the reception and give 'em something to talk about?"

It was tempting. Made even more so by the warmth radiating up her arm from Nate's casual touch. She didn't want it to end, but as he led her out into the kitchen access hall Payton's steps dragged.

Nate turned, seemingly amused by her hesitance. "What?"

"I need to think about this."

The idea of the talk surrounding her laced with something other than pity was thrilling, and the opportunity to spend some time with Nate again—well, she didn't quite know how she felt about that. If it was even possible for her to pretend to have a relationship with him at the same time she was pretending her attraction wasn't sincere. What she did know was that Nate wasn't a man to ask for favors lightly.

He *needed* her.

Still, a decision of this magnitude deserved at least one night's consideration. "Give me the evening and I'll call you tomorrow."

Ahead the door to the ballroom opened a crack as a waiter or someone prepared to back through it. Payton took a step in retreat, only to have Nate draw her to a stop.

"Here's the thing, Payton." His blue eyes had her now, cool and deep and dangerous. Captivating. "I've already thought about it. This is a prime opportunity and the results will benefit us both."

He'd already— "What?"

His loose grasp on her hand shifted, tightened as though he thought she might bolt. "Trust me," he urged in a tone of pure seductive persuasion.

Her chin shot up. She'd known Nate back when he was cultivating that tone and, while she couldn't say she was exactly immune, she wasn't wholly susceptible either. "No."

He could forget about luring her in the way he did every other man, woman and child on the planet. She knew how he operated and the last thing she needed was another overbearing man trying to control her.

She wasn't one of his devotees—some Wall Street junkie determined to live as Nate lived and follow in the footsteps of the financially infallible. And she wasn't one of his bimbos either, hanging on his arm and every whim. She was Payton Liss, determined to secure her independence, and she wasn't giving into this man just because his voice stroked like rough velvet over her every independent thought!

The corner of his mouth quirked up a degree and something

about his smile, one she'd seen countless times before and knew promised pure mayhem, put all her senses on alert. Her stomach jumped and she tried to escape.

"Oh, no, you don't," she gasped, backing down the hall with Nate matching her step for step, still holding her hands captive within his. She glanced over her shoulder, and nervous laughter erupted with the realization she'd somehow ended up moving toward the ballroom rather than away. *Stupid.*

"Come on...trust me."

That grin!

"I *don't* trust you," she shot back, her pulse rocketing in response to the predatory intent blazing in his eyes. She'd be a fool to trust a man leering at her like that—as if she'd made his week with this little game of cat and mouse.

"You should," he cajoled, this time taking a step into her space. "I've got a knack for making things work."

Payton peered up at him as he drew her closer—to the point where their feet tangled, legs touched. He was so bad. So incredibly, *unrepentantly bad.*

"You're arrogant," she accused, laughing as she nearly stumbled into his chest.

"You *like it,*" he challenged, with a pointed jut of his chin, just daring her denial. But, God help her, she couldn't. She'd always loved his crazy confidence. Nate's unwavering ability to fly in the face of convention and come out on top. He was free and, contrary to popular opinion, didn't take himself too seriously...so neither did she. Only, if Nate pulled her any closer, "serious" would become inevitable.

Her hands moved ineffectually to his chest. "What are you—?"

But then the door to the ballroom pushed fully open and, with an expertly maneuvered tug, Nate caught her up against the hard-cut planes of his body in a hold so provocatively intense she couldn't think of anything beyond the miracle of its fit. Ice-blue eyes slid over her in a chilling caress that left her skin pebbled with goose bumps.

Flashing a quick wink, he caught the back of her neck. "Trust me. I've done this before."

Lips parted in protest, Payton didn't manage a word before he moved in and, with deadly accuracy, captured her mouth beneath his.

CHAPTER THREE

THE kiss was blatant and intense, a showy play of passion that bowed her in a delicate arch, caged by the unyielding iron and steel of Nate's powerful frame. Firm, smooth lips moved over hers in a back and forth rub so skillfully seductive she could only sigh under their assault. Give into the idea that, if she wasn't going to escape the spotlight as she'd planned, there were plenty worse things than being exposed while discovering what it was to be kissed by Nate Evans.

It was *all consuming.*

There was something undeniable in his touch, something chemical, instinctual and wholly unexpected. She didn't understand it—couldn't defend against it as, locked in his hold, her body and mind pushed into overdrive.

Eyes closed, fingers flared at his shoulders, she tried to brace against the curl of anticipation licking through her belly. Remind herself that Nate's mouth sliding against her own was just for show. For whomever had opened the ballroom door—the door that remained open if the volume of the music spilling into the hallway around them was any indicator. It was a kiss for the gossips. For their individual self-serving interests. But not for their hearts or souls or even their libidos. Only the deafening rush of blood speeding past her ears—the heat of it surging through her veins, awakening her body in ways she couldn't deny—suggested otherwise.

Any second he would stop. Pull away and take this fantasy, a lifetime in the making, with him. But until then...

Payton clutched at the hand-stitched lapels of his jacket, her body curving into his. She'd call it a good show, call it anything Nate needed to hear, but the honest truth was no fantasy had ever measured up to this moment and, audience or not, she couldn't control her physical reaction to a kiss she'd dreamed of since she was thirteen.

Her fingers skimmed over the contours of his broad shoulders, following the column of his neck until they threaded into the thick silk of the curls at the base of his skull. The forbidden luxury of her hands in his hair, coupled with the seductive pull of his mouth against her own, was too much— too good, everything and not enough all at once—and drove a soft, pleading moan past her lips.

Nate stilled, his mouth fused with hers.

Oh, no, he'd heard her. Heard the sound of desire in a kiss scripted for deceit. She couldn't move, couldn't breathe— couldn't quell the frantic beating of her heart or her desperation to take this insanity further.

And then a breath, warm and wet, slipped between her suspended lips, carrying the gruff response to her needy plea. "Payton."

Tension charged the air around them, a current jumping from each point of contact to the next.

What was this?

The arms that held her circled tighter, slipping into something wholly different than the embrace of a moment ago. Into a slow, sensual exploration of his hands across her body.

Heat radiated from his touch like a hot claim, waking her every nerve. Every sense. Every desire.

She needed to stop.

Nate obviously read her renegade moan as a call to spur him further. To up the charade. Only Payton was already in over her head. Her body couldn't decipher the real from the imitation. And—as his tongue licked at the corner of her lips, eliciting a shudder that racked her from top to toe, had her opening wider to the exquisite sensation of Nate Evans seducing her with his mouth, his tongue, his teeth, and the soft rumble of his groan sounding between them—she slipped beneath reason, drowning in need. She wanted him. More than his kiss. She wanted everything he could give her, show her.

Only, already it was ending. His lips eased from hers by degrees until only the barest brush of skin and breath kept contact. That lingering touch, suggesting he, too, was hesitant to break away.

A kiss so carnal, so hot, couldn't have been—

Don't be stupid. Of course, it could.

She was dealing with notorious Nate, playboy extraordinaire and on a worldwide scale as she heard it. She was out of her league. Out of her mind. And potentially spoiled for life because of one insane, staged make out she hadn't had the sense of self-preservation to defend against.

But Nate had caught her off guard. And within the decadent span of that kiss, every fine strand of lingering attraction toward the boy he'd been wove and wound itself into an indestructible tether to the man he was now.

Oh, she was in such trouble.

Breath ragged, she tried to focus on the shadowed planes of the face only inches above her. Taking in the harsh drawn features she knew so well—the strong cut of his jaw, chiseled lips, that once-broken nose—she couldn't bring herself to meet his eyes. To see his thoughts or risk he'd see hers.

Gaze fixed on the breadth of the shoulders shielding her from the reception, she waited for him to step back and reveal his latest conquest. Then it would be over.

Only she didn't want the seduction to end.

Her hands slipped down to his chest, palms pressed flat against the definition of pure masculine form. If he could sneak up on her like that, she could grope him a bit while she got her breath back. It was only fair. Except the feel of his hard-packed physique beneath her hands wasn't doing much to calm her. The flex and pull of his layered muscles. The beads of his nipples. Hard and enticing. Forbidden little playthings that, once found, she couldn't leave alone.

Nate's hands clamped around her wrists, stilling her shameless exploration as his breath punched out in a cough.

What a fool to think this could be hers.

Pulling herself together, she managed to make light of a situation that was anything but. "You could have warned me," she laughed, praying the sound was more convincing than it felt.

A second passed. And then another. Her eyes closed against the rising ache in her chest. The crazy sense of despair she didn't have any right to. She wanted more. Wanted to be the kind of woman a man like Nate took home. But he'd already said it once. She was the good girl.

He took her chin between his finger and thumb. Her gaze lifted to his and her breath caught. Strain deepened the lines etched around his mouth and blatant hunger darkened his eyes. His jaw jumped with a tension she couldn't believe.

"Warned you? No." His gruff voice was low and serious, not the jovial Nate she knew so well. He held her gaze, considering, and then slowly the corner of his mouth turned up. And closing the distance between them, he answered, "I don't think I could have."

Hell, this was Payton Liss twining her arms around his neck, melting into his kiss with a breathy sigh—a sound that was all sex and need, and doing very bad things to his imagination. Brandt's little sister whose grown-up curves burned against his body, heating his blood like liquid fire. Miss Off-

Limits herself, with her fingers wound tight in his hair, opening that lush mouth of hers in a sweetly seductive invitation, begging him to take. And he wanted to take. To hell with however many sets of eyes were trained on them through the open door at the end of the hall.

Except, as of that moment, Nate didn't want to share.

He didn't want to play pretend. He didn't want anything but the private continuation of the kiss that just blew his mind. There had to be a hundred reasons why giving into the need surging through his veins was a bad idea. Only, he couldn't think of one. All he could see, and with a sudden, vivid clarity, was that Payton Liss belonged in his bed.

The music faded, quieting to a muffled hum that resonated through the hallway around them.

Straightening, Nate shot a glance over his shoulder. The door to the ballroom had closed—whoever opened it having come, seen their fill and left. Whether they'd recognized Payton he had no idea, but they'd seen someone in a rather conspicuous dress. Which was enough for today.

His focus turned back to the unexpected lure in his arms, his gaze touching on each delicate feature of her upturned face. Lingering on her mouth as the brush of his thumb across her kiss-swollen bottom lip set off an all too satisfying shudder.

He wanted her. As he couldn't remember wanting before. And she was willing, in his arms, looking up at him with eyes asking for one thing. *More*.

Only with a woman like Payton, *more* could mean *way more* than what he had to offer. She didn't know the score and didn't play for fun. He couldn't risk her reading promises he had no intention of delivering on into the kiss they'd just shared.

"You know I'm not the right kind of guy for you, Payton."

It was a warning. Plain and simple. To both of them.

One he fully expected her to heed.

"Maybe I don't want the 'right kind of guy'." She swallowed, the color rushing to her cheeks as she held his stare. "Maybe, this once, I want the kind of guy who can give me a night no one else would dare."

CHAPTER FOUR

HER words shot like an electric current straight to his groin. Nate was a man accustomed to taking what he wanted, how he wanted it. Because of who Payton was, he'd been willing to exercise more restraint than he ever did. But with that soft-spoken gauntlet thrown, there was no going back. "Then we need to get out of this hall. Now."

Her eyes lit, the seductive curve of her lips stretching as she reached for his lapel, urging him back toward her storage closet. "The nest."

He let out a bark of disbelieving laughter and stopped her with a firm hold at her wrist. Spun her back with a tug. "Not a chance, princess. For what no one else would dare...we're going to want a bed to land on."

With that promise hanging between them, he grabbed her hand and pulled her toward the kitchen doors just as a busboy stepped out pushing an empty clearing cart. Nate caught him and slapped a fifty with his business card into the kid's palm. "Get your manager and tell him I want the best room you've got...in the next five minutes."

Four and a half minutes later they were alone in the Executive Suite, Payton's toes breezing inches above the carpet as Nate crossed to the bedroom, his mouth covering hers in an urgent, possessive claim staked with tongue and teeth and lips. Suspended in his hold, she caught the dizzying spin of the room from the corner of her eye an instant before her shoulders met the damask.

Oh, God, yes. They were feet from a bed and Nate had backed her against a wall instead.

Heart slamming, her fingers balled in the fabric of his shirt as she opened to the slow thrust of his tongue. Followed the measured retreat. And moaned as he thrust again, her body flaming to life with the knowledge this was real. More than some fantasy. More than a charade. Her every sense heightened and homed in on him, drowning her in the taste, touch and smell of *Nate*. The sound of his ragged breath. The look of hunger in his eyes before he went to her throat—his mouth devouring the sensitive spot where neck sloped into shoulder with an assault of gentle suction and grazing teeth, swirling tongue and hot, wet breath that infused every cell of her being with sensual achiness.

His hands covered her breasts in a kneading caress and then, fingers curling into the neckline of her dress, he pulled the fabric down, releasing them to perch atop the bunched taffeta. Groaning with pure male satisfaction, he pressed his mouth to the top of one mound and then the other, making her feel as though she were the gift to him, rather than the other way around.

"You're so soft."

And he was hard, every bit of him firm and taut, solid-packed man making her feel like a fragile doll in his grasp. This was the man of her every forbidden fantasy, exceeding them all with his kiss alone. This was Nate. And there was no way that kiss was as good as it got.

"Please," she gasped, asking for more of something she couldn't imagine but knew he could give.

"Please?" he growled, lips caressing the swell of her breast, the wet trail of his tongue miraculously teasing cool and searing hot in equal measure.

"Please, I want you." For so long and for so many reasons.

His head lifted and she saw the challenge rising, the glint of seductive mischief blazing in the blue of his eyes. "Just me?" he taunted, his hands sliding down her hips, over the curve of her bottom to the backs of her thighs. "Or me...doing things no one else would dare?"

Her breath caught, her lips parting for a response she couldn't fathom. And somehow, amid the overwhelming desire and surging lust, a whisper of delighted laughter slipped free.

How could she be laughing when her body was about to burst into flames? She'd never known a seduction like this. Never thought it could be playful and exciting and hot and insane all at once. But then she'd never been with Nate. And thinking about the man whose mouth should be classified as a weapon of mass destruction, she realized he was all of those things and more.

She didn't know what to expect from a night with him, particularly one he seemed to have taken as a challenge. Or exactly how far out of her league she was. All she knew was no man had ever looked at her the way he was looking at that moment. As if there was no part of her he wouldn't possess.

And God help her, she wanted him to have her. "Yes."

Hands slipping down the contours of his chest, over the ridged terrain of his abs, she curled her fingers beneath his cummerbund.

"Yes, she says," he chuckled gruffly, the hands at the backs of her thighs fisting in the excess fabric of her skirt. Lifting. Handful above gathered handful, until the heat of his palms covered her bare skin. "I used to think those curls of yours were the only untamed things about you. But it's not true." He licked and sucked at the tender swells, making them plump with his attentions. "You're wild."

A surge of pleasure having nothing to do with sex shot through her at his statement. Simple confirmation of what she'd hoped, needed to believe all along. He could see her—who she really was—when no one else had even thought to look. He was the only one.

She needed him, just one person who didn't get swept up in the tide of lies and rumors, the sea of untruths that even she perpetuated. One person who saw the faulted, fallible girl hiding behind all the muted perfection and stifling 'right' choices. He hadn't judged. Hadn't told. Hadn't done anything but laugh or chuck her under the chin when the real girl behind the princess snuck out to visit him.

"You could always see me," she whispered as those big hands moved over her legs from back to front. Torturously close and painfully far from where she wanted him to be.

Nate took a knee, and, with the layers of tulle and taffeta bunched over his arms, slowly pushed the mess of it above her waist. "Good God, this is a lot of skirt." Skimming a hand up her leg, he found the scrap of her lingerie. Made an appreciative sound that had her body instantly responding.

"Without a lot beneath it." He caught her knee and hooked it over one broad shoulder, taking her weight in his hands as her balance shifted to her standing leg.

"Nate!" she protested, unfamiliar with such intimate vulnerability—but the only response from beneath her skirts was a shocking, open-mouthed kiss that burned through the fragile silk between them and stunned her silent. She hadn't been expecting it—she'd thought he'd slip her panties down and take her against the wall. That was as daring as her imagination had gotten, but this—she'd been totally unprepared for the mind-blowing effect of a man at his knees before her.

Her breath held through the first languid sweeps of his

tongue, then escaped on a cry at the teasing bite and soft nuzzle of a man whose powers of seduction knew no limits. Never had she dreamed of anything like the hot, wet sensation of Nate's forbidden kiss skillfully coaxing her along the path of pleasure. His hands covered her bottom, giving it a hot, firm grasp that started the slow slide of molten desire through her core. His tongue stroked with a gradual increase of pressure until something too long restrained pulled hard at the reins of her control. Her fingers clutched his shoulders, knotted into his hair then shot back again—seeking purchase, a hold, an anchor amid the rising tide of her lust.

"Oh, God!" she cried, sucking air in desperate gulps as her body coiled tight beneath his ministrations. "I don't…I can't…" Her hands flew to her face as her knee buckled. But Nate had her, took her weight in his arms as he moved with the rhythm of her hips. Sodden silk gave way beneath the press of his tongue at her entrance, a cruel tease that left her panting, pleading for a release just beyond her grasp. And then, with a low growl, he held her to him as his rough kiss took her over the edge and through the free fall of pleasured abandon.

Releasing her leg from his shoulder, he set her back to her feet.

Half dazed, she barely registered his long arms snaking around her back. Suddenly the catch of her gown was open and all that dress was slipping free into a pool of shimmering lavender at her feet—leaving her standing wide legged, in a pair of sodden, pearl silk panties and four-and-a-half-inch heels. It was crazy after everything that had happened, all she'd let him do already, but under the sudden exposure her arms moved instinctively to shield herself.

Nate leaned back on his knees, his brow creased with intensity born of desire, his gaze trailing hot across her skin.

"No." Brushing her hands aside, he stood before her, his chest rising and falling with the efforts of his restraint. Need raged in his eyes. Lines of strain bracketed his mouth. The corded muscles of his neck stood out in stark relief.

For her.

Her hands relaxed at her sides as she leaned back into the wall allowing this devastating man to look his fill.

And then she was in his arms, beneath the renewed assault of his kiss. His guttural response scoring her lips as he pulled her into the unmistakable hardness of his ready body. Wide, strong hands skimmed across her back, her hips, her thighs in a reckless exploration that left the surface of her skin tingling with a deep radiating awareness, pulsing into the very center of her. It was electric and erotically invasive. It was insanity, and with every passing second she gave in more.

"I want you…" Sensation shot through her, making control a thing of the past. "I've wanted you…for so long."

Nate let out a low groan, his hands tightening over the curves he'd once sworn never to touch.

For so long…

This was Payton. Brandt's little sister. With her wide-eyed innocent stare all but guaranteeing she'd fallen under the misconception he was someone she could trust. Not tonight, she couldn't. He couldn't look out for her best interests, not with those breathy moans and little teeth working at his ear while her bare breasts pressed against his shirt. Not with the taste of her sweet on his tongue.

But if she'd been carrying some kind of torch—

He couldn't ignore what everyone knew. She wanted the happily-ever-after. The down-on-one-knee, white-picket-fence, pram-around-the-park fantasy. And while most women wouldn't make the mistake of imagining him in that role, Payton had a bad habit of seeing him in ways no one else could. God only knew what she was thinking now. "We've got to stop," he gritted out. But the fingers at his waist only clenched tighter as her lust-clouded gaze drifted hungrily from his mouth to his eyes and back again.

"No," she gasped, reaching for him and sending his body into some kind of lust-induced free fall from rational ground.

No? He'd heard the word before. Could quite easily imagine it slipping past Payton's lips. Only the context was all wrong.

But then those soft lips were pulling at him, her breasts pushing against his chest and suddenly his hands were moving down the sleek line of her, settling over the bones at her hips and—

Damn it, he didn't want to stop. Didn't want to have to bring reason and rationale into something that was so good as pure instinct and response, but he wasn't a kid and he knew all too well about the consequences of diving headlong into a skirt he didn't belong in.

"Payton, wait," he managed, ignoring the wounded look in her eyes as he held her still. She needed to understand. "I'm not looking for marriage."

"Okay." She nodded, her gaze already targeting his mouth as she leaned into him again, making him wonder if she'd actually registered what he said at all. That was a risk he couldn't take. He set her back a pace, having to check that the woman driving him past sense was who he thought. Payton. Hot, demanding Payton, with her slight fingers brushing against his navel as she tried to get into his pants. Heaven help him.

"I'm serious. Look at me." Warm brown eyes, smoked with need, blinked wide as she peered up at him.

He wanted her so much it hurt. And yet, he still couldn't give in. Not yet.

"It's not just marriage. What's been going on with me— Payton, I can't do a relationship. I don't want one."

The pounding of his heart filled the seconds before she

answered. Something he didn't want to consider flickered in her eyes. Remorse. He knew better—but before he could drag his own ass outside to kick it, something new surfaced in her gaze. Resignation. Acceptance. And then the spark of what could only be described as clarity and determination.

"Do you want tonight?"

How could she even ask?

Yes, he wanted tonight. But tonight was all he wanted. Well, that and Payton not getting hurt. Just two consenting adults having a good time with no expectations. Only sometimes good girls like Payton got the wrong idea when they were making out with guys at weddings. Something about the tux triggered those saccharine fairy-tale fantasies and then suddenly they started attributing all kinds of meaning to an event that began as a little sordid groping in a back hallway. Sometimes they thought if they played along, things would change—the guy would change.

But he wouldn't. He *couldn't*. And he wasn't about to let Payton believe otherwise.

Only before he could open his mouth, she was pulling his face to meet hers. "Stop looking at me like I'm some little girl you have to protect." Her hands drifted lower, running down his chest to settle low at his abdomen again. "See me as the woman who wants a single night with you."

It couldn't be that easy. That straightforward. Except the stare meeting his own shone with an intent of purpose he couldn't mistake.

She wanted him and she understood this wasn't the beginning of forever.

It was tonight. He had one night—a mere handful of hours—to give her what no other man would dare to.

Oh, yeah.

No more second-guessing. No more wasted time.

Sweeping Payton into his arms, he strode to the bed and

tossed her—wide eyed and squeaking—back into the pillows. Followed her down, getting off on the fact he had her naked but for a scrap of silk and those incredible heels that were driving him nuts…and he was still decked out in the full tux minus the jacket. That worked for about two seconds before he was backing off the bed, taking those tiny panties with him. He wanted inside her more than he wanted to revel in some fantasy.

Working the studs free, he had his shirt half off before the sound of her voice halted his actions. "Nate?"

His head snapped up to where Payton lay reclined, one knee sliding slowly against the other. Fighting past the rise of pure lust at the vision of her there for his taking, he sent up a silent prayer she hadn't come to her senses. "What?"

The pink tip of her tongue slipped in a moist trail across the swell of her bottom lip. "Hurry."

He swallowed hard. The shirt came off in a spray of onyx studs clattering against whatever surfaces they reached, followed immediately by the cummerbund, pants and the rest. Body taut with need, he rolled on a condom retrieved from his pants, unwilling to be careless with either of their futures, and then he was on her again, losing himself in the feel of her mouth, the press of her breasts and the glide of her knee against his hip as she melted in his arms.

It was torture, but he held himself in check as he pressed his length at her entrance. His gaze holding hers, silently offering one last chance to change her mind.

Maybe it was all the memories he had tied up with her. Or that he couldn't quite stop thinking of her as the girl he wanted to protect from the guys like him. But whatever nonsense he'd let take seed in his mind, Payton swept it away with one head-back, body-arched gasp of pure need…

"Please." And then as though that weren't enough, "Ye-e-e-s-s-s," when he began to move.

Oh, yeah, he liked the sound of that at his ear as he pushed into the tight clasp of her body. Too tight to thrust hard, he gritted his teeth through the measured penetration, pulled back, only to sink again, slowly taking her deep and then deeper still, repeating again and again until he was buried to the hilt.

Her lips were parted, a suspended breath hanging between them. Looking into her eyes, he held, lost in something too good. Too perfect a fit. Too intensely right.

Her body gripped him with the rhythmic pulse that signaled she was close, and his jaw clenched hard in his fight for control. He followed her every gasp and sigh, learning exactly what she liked, what made her crazy. And when those delicate hands moved down his body, from his shoulders to his arms to his back, clutching at him as if she needed to hold on…it satisfied him in a way he didn't even want to contemplate.

She was incredible. Coming apart in his arms even as she begged him for more.

Hell, yes, there was more. A whole night's worth of more. Payton didn't want to be the good girl tonight, and after six months he needed to be bad.

CHAPTER FIVE

PAYTON roused herself from a sated state of lethargy, peeling back her eyelids only to encounter a tangle of curls blocking her view. Shifting slowly, she reached up to shove the mess from her eyes—halting at the slow rise and fall of a chest beneath her cheek.

Nate.

She swallowed down the burst of joyous excitement as images, sensations and whispers of the night before bombarded her waking consciousness.

He'd been so gentle with her the first time. So careful. And then after that—

Her toes curled deep beneath the sheets at the thought of all they'd done.

Everything.

They'd made love, over and over again. Nate waking her with his hands, his mouth. A seductive growl accompanied by his rising need. Nothing planned. Nothing proper or polite about it.

Incredible.

"What's got you smiling so early?" Nate's morning-rough voice stroked over her like a soothing caress, bringing her attention to the hard line of his stubbled jaw and the soft amusement in his blue, blue eyes. They were intimately wound together. Arms and legs and bare skin everywhere. It felt good and, though today they wouldn't be lovers, Payton wasn't about to rush from the bed or give up the warmth of his body, the steady *thump, thump* of his heart sounding beneath her ear, or the shelter of his arms around her. She couldn't. Not yet.

For now, they were comfortably entwined. Or at least they were until Nate reached down her back with one hand and pinched her bottom.

"Hey!" she squeaked, ineffectually trying to pinch back at skin too muscle packed to give.

"The grin. Tell."

Inching her bum out of pinching distance, she raised a brow. "So desperate to feed your ego?"

"Mmm, so it's an ego-feeding grin. Tell me more."

She took a deep breath, weighing the temptation to share her indecent revelation. He'd never judged her before…but this was different. Telling in a way she wanted him to know but was afraid to reveal. After what they'd done last night, she might have finally killed the *good girl* misconception, and owning up to what had her smiling—the part beyond finally being in his arms—might negate all the progress she'd made. Casting a sidelong glance his way, to that devilish smile and waiting stare, the temptation proved too much to resist. Her eyes squeezed shut and she fessed up in a rush of breath. "I'm thinking you're the first notch in my bedpost."

There! That wasn't so bad. It was freeing, in fact. And—

Her eyes blinked open as Nate froze beside her, every muscle in his body gone taut and his breathing at an abrupt halt.

Her chin pulled back. Not quite the "partner-in-crime" kind of response she'd hoped for.

He couldn't be *insulted*. But now that she thought about it, she wouldn't feel great about being described as a notch either.

"You weren't a virgin." The words rasped out more plea than question or statement.

Momentarily stunned, Payton could practically feel his cold dread at the thought she'd saved something so special for him. That the night he'd given her on condition it be casual be so spectacularly significant. That she'd deceived him.

"No!" Her hands flew to the sides of her face as she shook her head in vehement denial. "I wasn't a virgin, I promise! I meant 'notch' like uncommitted. Sex for sex's sake." The beginning of her reckless adventure. He didn't need to know how special being with him truly was to her. After today it would never be an issue again. She wouldn't let it be. "Don't panic, please."

Nate's relief was a palpable thing, like a rush of air back into the room, the return of pressure with a whoosh.

"I wasn't panicking," he scoffed, pushing to one elbow on his side. "Pretty little princesses don't make me panic. Especially not when they are…" he lifted the sheet for dramatic effect, offering a quick leer at her prone body before meeting her eyes again "…naked."

Relief washed through her at the ease with which he recovered, but a lingering tension remained and his expression turned serious. Concerned.

"Are you okay about this, Payton?" Catching a wild curl with his finger, he pushed it over her ear. Let his mouth pull into a crooked twist when it sprang free and bounced back in front of her eyes. "With last night being the only night?"

She took a steadying breath. "I am if we go forward as friends."

In those first minutes after the kiss became real in the hallway, she might have indulged in a fantasy where there could be more. A little longing or hope. But she'd quickly understood it wasn't a romance in the making. And though a part of her cared for Nate on a level she couldn't acknowledge to him, there was another part of her excited by the raw rush of her very own too-good-to-feel-guilty-about night of passion. A night only he could give her. Because she trusted him.

"Friends," he said as if testing the word out.

"Yeah. I've missed you in my life. I don't want to give you up again."

Tiny lines etched at the corners of his eyes as he held her stare. "Do you feel like you can go forward from here without this—" he waved a slow hand between them "—getting in the way?"

She knew she could. She'd done it for years before Nate walked out of her life. "I can if you can. Even if you can't tell if you've got a virgin in your bed."

Brows arching high as he let out a sharp laugh, Nate rocked back, pulling Payton over with him. "Be a while before I live that down, will it?"

She squinted at him from her perch atop his chest. "Probably."

"Then I better steer this little chat back toward the ego feeding." Settling against the pillow to get comfortable, he prompted, "So tell me how it is I score bedpost-notch status."

Payton readjusted around him and let her gaze run the length of his pure masculine perfection, complete with one heavily muscled leg thrown over the sheet, and wondered how he could even ask.

"It's just it was so…intense without being…serious. It wasn't candlelight and promises of love everlasting."

"You don't like those things?" he asked, running a finger down the curve of her shoulder.

Guiltily she glanced away, then forced her gaze back. "No, I do. I'm sure I would—" If she ever actually felt that forever kind of glow, she would probably love it. If Nate had wanted to give her those things…

Only he didn't and she knew it. The only thing everlasting

in their future was the schoolgirl crush she expected would never quite go away. And a friendship if she was lucky. "What I mean is this was so…*hot* and it's never been like that for me before. Impulsive. Exciting." She felt the blush creeping into her cheeks—held Nate's gaze anyway, needing him to understand. "No strings. No expectations."

"Hell, if I'd known that I wouldn't have worked so hard."

She let out her own laugh then, swatting harmlessly at his chest. "You know what kind of expectations I'm talking about. The long-term kind." It would be impossible to go to bed with Nate without some kind of expectation. His name was practically scrawled on the ladies' lounge wall next to the words "for a good time". "It's never been so much…fun. So…free. My other experience wasn't like this."

This time it was Nate's turn to pull back. "Your 'other experience'? As in singular? I mean, I knew your experience was limited, but that idiot was your first?"

"Nate! Can't you at least pretend you don't know who I'm talking about? And he isn't an idiot." Clint wasn't perfect. Far from it. What she'd had with him was polite. It was pleasant. But it hadn't been deep and it hadn't been passionate. It hadn't been *real*. How could it have been when one of the people in the relationship hadn't actually existed? Not that Clint ever noticed or cared. But even so, it hardly seemed fair to discuss his lack of creativity and vigor with a man so completely out of his league.

"I can't believe you gave it up to *Clint*."

Payton bristled. Some long-ago disappointment—frustrated and immature—reared its head, lashing out. "Well, you didn't take it," she snapped. "I had to give it to someone."

Nate coughed, his brows crashing down. "Thankfully you never offered."

Yes, probably a good thing since he'd vanished from her life a few days after she'd decided she wanted him to be the one. She'd finally been ready to screw up the courage and tell him how she felt. Only it was too late. The friendship between them had become a casualty of the fallout with Brandt.

Nate's finger caught under her chin, urging her focus back to his face. "I think it might have killed me to say no. But I would have had to. You were sixteen."

"You were only eighteen."

"Yeah, but there's a big difference between those ages, Payton. Besides, I was leaving for school and I didn't ever want to come back."

Because of people like her brother and his friends. Nate knew plenty about being on the wrong side of the talk, just as she did. And right now, she didn't want either of them to have to think about it.

"Well, I suppose you might have been worth waiting for."

Propping an arm behind his head, he cocked a wry smile at her. "So glad you enjoyed yourself."

"The way my life has been going, well, I needed this— you." She blinked up at him, those soft brown eyes tugging at his heart just as they always had. "You really are quite a lot of fun."

Leaning in, he caught her lips with his own. His arm tightened across her back, holding her close through this soft, lingering last kiss. Slowly they parted and Payton let out a sigh that feathered over his jaw and neck as she drew away. It was a sweet, quietly satisfied sound that, coupled with the soft press of her breast against his abdomen, the smooth skin of her thigh crossed over his, and the bare heat of her against him, had him fighting the urge to pull her back.

She felt good and he wanted her again. Wanted more fun. More intensity. He wanted to give her more of what she'd never had before. Except he didn't want to give her any kind of false promise or misconception about the potential for a relationship. And something in those big brown eyes staring up at him said he needed to tread carefully. Payton's heart was a responsibility he didn't want to bear.

"I get what you're saying. And I had a good time, too." "Had" being the operative word.

"Thanks, Nate." Her grin spread wide and she closed her eyes indulging in one long, languorous stretch that moved her in a slow slide of flesh as she rolled away from him. His gut tensed as she arched back, rotating her hips in a decadent extension of feminine musculature and pretty pink skin. He should look away. Turn his head. Get the hell out of the bed before he did something stupid, but already his heart was turning over, getting ready to rev with thoughts of consequence quickly dissipating.

Maybe just one more—

And then she was climbing out of bed—dragging the sheet he'd barely had a corner of with her as she cast an impish wink back and darted for the bathroom.

His fingers tingled where he'd almost gotten hold of her. Damn, it was a good thing they were taking this off a physical level. He liked control. After the past six months, he needed it. And Payton, all naked and soft, had an unnerving ability to threaten his.

He glared at the closed bathroom door. He wasn't following her in there.

The shower sounded, then the quiet thud of the sliding glass door as it closed.

He wasn't going to take her against the tile wall. Bury himself inside her again. No. Because if he gave in, one more time wouldn't be enough. It would be again and again. Finding new and creative ways to get Payton's petite form wrapped tight around him. In his arms. In his bed. But that was all he'd have to offer her. Sex. And right now, the friendship they both needed was more important than that.

So, no. Definitely not. He wouldn't follow.

CHAPTER SIX

PAYTON stood beneath the hot spray, her body tender from sensual satisfaction, her mind whirling a mile a minute as she began to compartmentalize everything that had happened with Nate. Everything that would happen. She needed to be cool, to make sure he understood she didn't have expectations about a future together. Or at least a romantic future. Because while last night had been incredible—exciting in a way she hadn't believed possible and would never regret—it was the going forward that mattered.

Going forward as friends.

Tipping her face beneath the water, she pushed back the sodden curls, wringing the heavy mass clean.

These past hours with Nate had been a taste of what she'd missed so much over the years. Someone who could see her as she truly was. Accept her without recrimination. He hadn't balked at her attraction—her interest in a single night of insanity. He'd helped her embrace it.

She needed that kind of freedom and acceptance as she edged out of the mold of perfect daughter to a man no longer there to maintain it for. She needed to be real.

Brandt wouldn't approve of this business with Nate, and her mother—well, she was already worried out of her mind about the changes Payton had made with her career, her apartment, Clint. Most of all Clint. Nate would be just one more thing.

But it was time she stopped living her life to someone else's expectations.

Turning the brass tap fixtures to "off", she stepped from the shower and knotted a thick terry bath sheet between her breasts. Stared into the mirror seeing the foggy image of a woman no one knew.

She'd been alone for too long. Surrounded by so many people—all the right people with their picture-perfect smiles and placid conversation—yet none of them knew her. What she really thought. Who she was.

And at the first sign she might be more than they believed, the talk had started. Concerned talk. Catty talk. The kind of talk she'd never been interested in and didn't care to listen to now. She'd rather be alone. Only eventually loneliness wore on a person and they started to search for someone—a friend—to take them as they were.

A breath eased from her chest. A smile curved her lips.

She'd found Nate. And he'd asked her to be the friend he needed. When she needed one most. So this would work.

She opened the bathroom door and stepped into the now sun drenched suite, scanning the floor for her panties and bra. And her dress! She didn't want to put that thing on again, but unless she planned to sprint for Nate's limo in a robe it was the only option.

They'd started by the wall, but the floor was clear. Then the bed—

Her lips parted in silent awe.

Nate sat reclined against the headboard in his black trousers and bare feet, hair a spiky mess and tuxedo shirt hanging open down his chest. His attention fixed on *The Wall Street Journal* in his hands.

The look was all sin and seduction and wild bad-boy. This was the shot the magazine should have run next to his most-wanted bachelor bio. He wouldn't be able to beat the women off with a stick.

Forcing her gaze away before he needed the stick for her, she noticed the pink lounge pants, zip jacket and shirt neatly folded at the foot of the bed. An accompanying set of lacey panties and bra lay beside them. "When— How?"

Without looking up, he yawned, "While you were in the shower."

She checked the tags. This man had practice purchasing women's clothing. "Quite an impressive skill set you have going on—your ability to guess sizes so accurately."

A wry smile tugged at his lips. "I've got my limitations. I'd've had a tough time eyeballing you for a fitting. But I know exactly what fills my palm."

"You're bad," she muttered, running a fingertip over the soft fabric.

"Yeah, but, as we've already established…" he folded the paper and tossed it beside him "…you like it." Rising from the bed, he cast a lazy glance her way—and stopped. His eyes riveted to her.

"What?" Her hands went to her hair, seeking out some pile of suds she'd missed. Then, tucking her chin, she looked down. Everything packed away where it was supposed to be, and yet Nate's halted posture—his unsettled reaction—was clearly in response to her. "Is something wrong?"

And then she saw it, in the last second before he gave an abrupt shake of the head and turned his back to her.

Heat. Desire. Ruthlessly shut down. She understood they weren't continuing a physical relationship, but his almost hostile reaction—

"Nate?" she asked, crossing her arms over her chest to stave off the cool chill running through her heart.

"Nothing. Just realized I forgot a file at the office," he

answered abruptly. "Go on and get dressed and we'll get out of here."

Payton took a step back. "Sure. Of course." Just as well. She'd been looking at Nate like too much of a temptation anyway and that wasn't going to work. Not for either of them. Gathering the loungewear he'd gotten for her, she went back to the bathroom. The sooner they got out of this suite and back onto solid friendship ground, the better.

A few minutes later she returned to find a hastily scrawled note atop the bed.

Had to rush out. My driver is waiting for you downstairs. I'll get your address and stop over this afternoon.

Payton stared down at the note in blatant disbelief. She'd been on the other side of the door, a few panels of wood between then, and he'd left a note? The nerve!

No—this was something other than nerve. Nate would never intentionally hurt her. He might cat around, but he wasn't cruel and he wasn't callous. Her mind played back the minutes before he'd left, slowing to that last glimpse of desire and then anger. He hadn't wanted to see her that way. Hadn't wanted the attraction.

So be it. She'd look at this as the clean break they needed.

When she saw him again, it would be as friends.

And then her *friend* could explain what kind of a mess he'd gotten himself into that he needed a pretend affair to cover it up.

Nate raked his fingers through his hair, balling them at the base of his skull before letting go with a grunt. His dogged strides ate up the sidewalk, taking him fast from the scene of the crime. He was a jackass of the most contemptible variety.

But seeing her there, wrapped in that towel, wet tendrils of hair snaking over her bare shoulders, tiny beads of water sprinkled across the swells of her freshly scrubbed skin—it was like being thrown back in time. To a place he didn't want to revisit.

To a time when he was still mere potential and promise. Trying to exist within the confines of an environment that wanted to squelch the pride and drive out of him. Teach him a lesson. Show him he wasn't good enough. That nothing he did could change it.

When all the frustrations and inequities of his youth came to a head—all driven by one inadvertent mistake. One look. One girl.

And like that, the years folded over and his feet were pounding up the stairs at the Liss house as he went for the textbook he'd left on Brandt's floor the night before. Breaking the landing, he'd looked up, and through the open door of Payton's bedroom, there she was. Brandt's little sister emerging from her bathroom—fresh from the shower. Totally unaware.

He stopped breathing. Stood, mouth agape, stunned. Payton, his little shadow—always bundled in those conservative sweaters, jackets and formless clothing, her hair restrained, her legs covered—stood wrapped in a towel, her curls wet and wild, her curves unmistakable, her legs bare and pink and looking so soft. He jerked his gaze away. Snapped his jaw shut and forced his fists into his pockets.

God help him, she was beautiful. Hell, he'd known she was beautiful. Sweet and funny. But he'd never wanted her until that very minute and it caught him like a sock to the gut.

For too many reasons he had to get out of there. Couldn't risk that he'd look again.

Turning, he opened his eyes to the enraged red of Brandt's face. And in that instant the façade of forced civility between them crumbled and the cold truth glared back at him.

Hatred.

Nate had always been aware of the barely contained aggression simmering beneath the surface with Brandt. It wound the kid off to no end to be dependent on a guy he considered his inferior for the tutoring that put the Ivy League school so necessary to his elitist identity within reach. There'd always been a cool distance. The laughingly misplaced attitude Brandt was the one doing Nate a favor, rather than the other way around. Yeah, Nate had gotten paid—he sure as hell hadn't spent four afternoons a week for three years waiting on Brandt to get off the phone or bother to show up out of friendship. But still, he hadn't expected the depth of loathing he now saw.

"Take it easy. It's not what you think—"

"Bull! You were staring at her." A hand shot out, shoving hard at Nate's shoulder. "I saw your damn face, man. You aren't good enough for her. Not even to look!"

Nate didn't take to being pushed around. Not by anybody, but Payton was Brandt's little sister. So, rather than knocking the guy's head back with the punch gathering in his fist, he reached out and hauled him down the stairs and out to the front yard. Away from Payton. "You're off base. I was leaving."

"Damn straight you are," Brandt sneered. "And you're nuts if you think you're ever coming back here."

"Fine, whatever." Let the Lisses deal with the fallout. The school year was nearly over anyway. He'd get another job, something to last through the summer until he got out of this inbred cesspool and into U of I. "Look, I was going for my Calc book upstairs. If you get it for me, I'll take off."

Brandt let out a snort, rocking back on his heels to look down his nose at Nate. "Yeah, I'll get right on that."

He looked up to the house. He needed that book and, after this, going to Payton wasn't an option either.

Brandt followed his eyes and let out a disgusted grunt. "What'd you think, with summer a few weeks off you needed another ticket onto the gravy train? That sniffing around my sister would get you back by the poolside?"

Screw him.

"Forget it, Evans, Payton's not like the rest of your dates. The girls who go out with trash to get back at their daddies."

Nate's blood, already hot, began to boil beneath the rise of a deep-seated pride held too long in check. It was absurd and he knew it. But still something in the jab stung. Hit a little too close to an insecurity he didn't want to acknowledge. A sense of alienation he couldn't quite get past. "Go to hell."

"After you. And here." Brandt went for his wallet and pulled out a stack of crisp bills. More money than Nate earned in a month. "For the cost of your book."

Extracting a fifty, Brandt dropped the bill to the dirt and ground it in with his heel. "Go ahead. Pick it up. You know you can't afford to replace it on your own."

Nate's muscles bunched, his knuckles whitened at his side as the world closed in around him. He had to get out of there. Forcing his legs to move, he turned. Took a step to leave.

It didn't matter. Brandt didn't matter.

But the kid wouldn't give it up and grabbed for him. "Hey, I'm not done with you yet."

"Don't be stupid, Liss," he warned, easily shaking the other boy off, determined to walk away.

"You calling me stupid?" Brandt grabbed again...cocking his arm as he spun Nate back.

Mistake. One too many...and then the blood was flowing fast and red before Nate even realized he'd thrown. Brandt staggered back a step, fell on his ass with a howl before finding his feet and running toward the house. "You're going to pay for that, Evans!"

Damn it, where was his control? Nate's heart slammed within his chest as the repercussions of his actions sped through his mind. Arrest, expulsion, college, his escape from a life he'd almost been free of. His dad could end up paying for this mistake. What the hell had he done?

The door to the Liss house flew open and Payton, now dressed in jeans and a turtleneck, rushed onto the lawn. Eyes wide with hurt disbelief, she stared down at Nate's knuckles and the smear of her brother's blood streaking them.

"I'm sorry." His voice was rough with emotion, shame and disgust. He should have known better. He'd been so close to escaping this place without giving into his own sense of injustice. And now this.

In the end, he hadn't been arrested. Hadn't paid any price beyond his own personal shame at allowing Brandt Liss to goad him into losing control. But that price had been enough.

Hell, it was crazy. One glimpse of Payton wrapped in her towel back in the suite and all the insults and accusations had sliced through time, cutting fresh into his mind. Stupid prejudices. Words he couldn't believe he'd let bother him.

So why had his gut tightened, as though controlled by unpleasant muscle memory? Why had his body instantly wound tight, setting for a fight? And why, beneath it all, was he still tied up by that single forbidden memory of Payton and the taunt of a guy whose significance to Nate's life barely registered?

Not good enough…not even to look…

Maybe. No, definitely. But sure as hell not for the reasons Brandt believed.

CHAPTER SEVEN

IT WAS close to two when the bell rang. Payton had spent the better part of the morning—what was left of it once she'd been dropped home—doing her best not to think about Nate and what would happen when they saw each other. How exactly one transitioned from lover to friend, and what it would take for her mind to stop playing out scenarios where she ended up back in his arms, beneath his kiss.

That was thinking she couldn't afford. So she'd done as little of it as possible.

But now her avoidance was at an end. Nate was downstairs. At her door. And all the thoughts she'd so effectively ignored were bombarding her at once.

Thoughts like spending the night together had been reckless. Careless. And might have irrevocably changed his feelings for her. Jeopardized their friendship by putting her on par with some nameless "double D" he'd picked up at a club.

Her anxiety rose with each step she descended until she swung open the security door, took in the vision of him—big and broad, dressed casually in weathered jeans, untucked oxford and a lightweight, ash V-neck sweater—and lost her breath to the enormous bouquet of yellow roses he held out in offering.

She fell back against the door, a hand going to her throat where emotion threatened to choke her. He'd brought her friendship flowers. The perfect transition from last night to today. A tender reassurance of the caring between them.

"Oh, you're good," she said, shaking her head in awe.

"What kind of greeting is that for your secret lover?" Nate asked, a smug smile on his face. "Shouldn't you be suspiciously glancing around and then dragging me inside before someone catches sight of us out here?"

"So back to the charade, then?" Trying to curb the grin that spread to her lips when she'd opened the door, she crossed her arms. "You're enjoying this way too much."

He cocked his head as if considering, then shrugged. "You might be right, but, the way I see it, it's a pretty good way to feed my fantasies. Just play like there's a crowd watching and I get a beautiful woman to heed my every command."

He thought she was *beautiful*. "Your every command, huh?"

"Mmm-hmm. Very kinky. The whole control thing. Sorry we didn't get around to it, but there's a limit to even my abilities within one night."

She couldn't help but laugh, wondering how it was that the world at large believed Nate Evans so frightening. She'd never met anyone who took *themselves* less seriously—while at the same time being so seriously driven to success. "So you've gone mad with power, have you?"

"Seems I have."

"Well, in that case…" She made an exaggerated show of peering down the sidewalk and street, first one way and then the other, before grabbing for Nate's shirt and towing him in through the security door. Then, casting him an impish wink, she asked, "Was it good for you? Because it was definitely good for me."

Nate's jaw set to the side as he shook his head. "Sassy thing." Then after a beat, "Are you really okay with this?"

If he led the way…yes. "I am. But before we tempt fate with another hallway, let's get upstairs."

Nate nodded, and then as he glanced around his brow furrowed. She saw the moment his surroundings registered. No flash, no glitter. Just aging tile flooring. A worn banister leading up a simple staircase.

"I figured you for a skyrise penthouse or something. With a fleet of round-the-clock security guards, closed-circuit monitored elevator. This place isn't what I expected."

She headed up the first flight, acting as though his observation hadn't struck a nerve. It was okay. He wasn't entirely off-base, just about twelve months too late.

"I moved in last year." A few weeks after her father passed away. She couldn't stand to live in the apartment he'd been renting for her—let alone afford it. And when she'd found this…well, it suited her.

Catching up, Nate grunted something unintelligible and she decided not to ask. She'd been hoping he'd see the building and understand she was supporting herself. Maybe respect her autonomy. But it didn't matter. He'd see soon enough she'd made herself a home.

Nate rounded the third landing working through the reasons why Payton Liss would live in an apartment like this. Real estate speculation? She'd bought the building and was living-in while she worked a refurb of some sort. But where was the telltale smell of construction? And why the third floor apartment and the hallway reeking of ethnic cuisine. "Something on the stove?"

She shook her head, drawing in a deep breath. "No, that's the Craines on two. I get hungry every time I walk past."

The single door on the third floor stood ajar, left open from when she'd run down to let him in, and two things struck him at once. The first, single women should never leave their apartment doors open. And the second, what the hell had she been running down to the first floor for—where was the security box to screen and admit her guests? Before he could ask, she swung the door open and, smiling wide, walked in.

To a shoe box.

Not even as big as the place he'd lived with his dad.

"What is this?" he demanded, hostility welling inexplicably within him.

"This is my apartment, Nate. And stop scowling at it like it's something you need to scrape off your shoe."

"But what are *you* doing living in it?" She had money, security. It didn't make sense.

She rounded on him with an open-mouthed expression of disbelief and maybe something worse.

He didn't care. "Where's the security intercom?"

"What?"

"It's not safe to leave your apartment and come down to check the security door. How do you even know who's out there? Someone could be waiting in the hall for you to open the door." She was so slight, so petite, she'd never stand a chance against an attacker. His aggravation flared.

Crossing to the front windows, he checked the latches and tested the frame. Secure enough, but—

"For your information, Nate, I like it. It's affordable, close to the school, the 'L' and the lakefront."

A glimpse out the window confirmed what he already suspected: a trip to the lakefront entailed taking the pedestrian underpass below Lake Shore Drive. He turned on her. "Tell me you don't walk over there by yourself."

She looked as though he'd slapped her, but if she didn't have sense enough to look out for herself, then she was going to have to put up with some pointed questions from him.

"Does Brandt even know about this?" Where the hell was her brother's protective instinct now? Her father was gone and that prick Clint had bailed. She needed someone looking out for her now more than ever.

"Yes. Brandt knows. I've had him to dinner once. Though, like you, he found it lacking and he prefers to take me out."

Found it lacking. That was for damn sure. So why hadn't he set her up somewhere more suitable? He knew for a fact Brandt just bought some office building downtown. There was money, so why was Payton living like a pauper? Maybe dropping in on Brandt at work would shed some light on it. He could put the priority of Payton's security into perspective for the guy.

No, forget it. Bad idea. He'd handle the situation himself. He didn't have time to be worrying about her safety.

"You can't live here. We'll find another apartment this afternoon."

Payton's back stiffened, and those earthy warm eyes that had been looking up at him as if he were the only man in the world mere hours ago took on a glare that said he was just another jerk. "What?"

The decision made, he pulled his phone from his pocket to call up a realtor he knew. "Don't worry about the rent."

But then Payton was in his face, her finger jabbing into his chest. "Have you lost your mind?" she snapped. "Of all the controlling, overbearing— I'm not moving out. I chose this place so I could have my *independence. I love it here.*"

He stared at her, comprehension dawning, but not quickly enough to stop the next barb. "When did you become such a damn snob, Nate?"

So she was paying her own way. He knew all too well about independence. The need for it having driven him to finish school early while working a job at the same time. Anything to get far enough ahead he wouldn't have to go back. But if she wasn't safe, it wasn't acceptable. "The intercom—"

"Is being replaced on Monday. And, not that it's any of your business, but I jog at the lakefront every morning and always carry pepper spray and an emergency air horn. The crime rate in the neighborhood is particularly low, my landlord's security precautions are high, and I don't appreciate your steamrolling one bit." Her arms were crossed, her breath coming fast with her frustration. But her eyes—beneath that sparking hostility he caught the glimpse of hurt and disappointment.

What was he doing?

This place was important to her and he'd stormed in and treated it like garbage. What was the matter with him? He'd taken one look, decided it didn't fit his idea of what Payton's life should be like and flown off the handle in what he could only explain as an overprotective, testosterone-driven mania.

"I'm being an ass. There's nothing wrong with your apartment." In fact, as he adjusted his perspective, he couldn't see anything wrong with it at all. It wasn't brand-new or extravagant, but it was clean. Neat. Cozy. The view was attractive, the light good. The design was old Chicago, with attractive molding and high ceilings throughout. Crystal-knob fixtures and etched-glass transoms. A brick hearth. Hardwood floors. The apartment was attractive. The furniture tasteful and conservative. Homey.

He simply hadn't expected to find Payton Liss living here. And for some reason, it irritated him that she did.

Arms still crossed, she shifted her weight from one hip to the other. Blew out a breath that sent a stray curl momentarily adrift, and then moved over to the couch and plopped down into the cushions. "You weren't much worse than Brandt. So, I suppose I'll have to forgive you."

Wow, not much worse than Brandt. He needed to spend more time with his dad if he'd become that much of a snob.

Nate glanced over to where she'd leaned into the cushioned armrest. An open paperback lay atop the coffee table beside her and a cup of tea that looked as though it had gone cool some time ago. He dropped into the opposite corner. It was comfortable. Good to be sitting with her. Only… He reached across and pulled Payton into him, tucking her under his shoulder, adjusting her just so as she laughed, not bothering to protest at all.

"Oh, yeah, that's it." Nice.

How many times had they sat like this as kids, watching TV, talking, joking around? How many times had he thought about it while wondering why another woman didn't fit quite as well? Payton was small boned and delicate, with all those sweet soft spots that made her fit just right.

After a minute of enjoying the familiarity, he rubbed a hand over her shoulder and leaned back to look at her. "I'm not trying to be insulting, but I've got to ask. What about your father's estate? I mean, the Lisses are wealthy."

She plucked a bit at the hem of her shirt before answering. "Honestly, my family is very generous and my mother would probably love to finance my every expenditure, but that kind of dependence comes with too many strings. I earn my own salary and…now that my father is gone, I prefer to pay my own way."

Ah-h-h. There it was. The mention of her father with the accompanying wince to go along. The visible twinge of guilt as though the admission that she was going against his wishes still pained her.

And yet she was doing it anyway. Changing her life.

With no rescue necessary, all he had to offer was the gentle squeeze of his hand over her shoulder. The quiet communication that he understood. And maybe a confidence of his own.

"We've got a date Tuesday night to stir up more press and gossip, but today's beautiful. What do you say we take a ride somewhere and talk?" Payton deserved to know what had spurred this whole fiasco. "Head down to the Dunes? We can work out the game plan for the month. Pace it out. And maybe just catch up some, too."

Her smile lit up the room. "Let me grab a sweater."

CHAPTER EIGHT

BENEATH the late September sky, Nate cut through the side streets, heading for Lake Shore Drive. Payton sat snuggled beside him in the sleek silver convertible, face tipped to catch the warm sunshine washing the city in an amber glow. The cold snap of a few days before coupled with the strong winds had blown half the autumn leaves from their trees in one quick drop. The result was a glorious quilt of toasted hues, alive with the wind, surging in swells and chasing the car in spirals of rusts and golds.

It was beautiful.

Nate grinned beside her. "Fall still your favorite time of year?"

"Yes. Though it isn't quite the same living in the city as it was back at the house."

"You miss raking?"

She glanced over. "Yeah, I do."

Brandt had thought she was nuts. She remembered his disdainful stare as he watched her sweeping the rake back and forth across the yard, pulling the accumulated leaves into mass, ignoring the burn in her shoulders until she had the pile as wide and tall as she was.

And then the surprise of strong hands grabbing her from behind, that wicked laugh coming a second before she was tossed into the pile.

"You always helped me."

He let out a short laugh. "Wasn't like Brandt would."

No. Nor her father. And Mom, she was more of Brandt's mind. Confused why her daughter would even look at a rake when the landscapers would mow, blow and pluck every fallen leaf from the yard each Friday.

They hadn't gotten it. But Nate had.

Payton closed her eyes, giving into the rush of open air around them as Nate blew south on the Drive headed for the Skyway. Her mind played in shadowed memories of leaf piles, Nate laughing at her side…and then as she drifted, lulled by the smooth hum of the engine, the memories became something else. A mix of then and now. A cross of memory and imagining blurred into one. The tastes and touches she'd only just learned coupling with their bodies rolling in a tangled embrace. The heavy weight of Nate pressing her down into a bed of crisp russet and plum foliage, the scent of woods and earth surrounding them.

His name broke her lips on a sigh. "Nate…"

"Yeah, babe?"

Payton jerked in her seat, the heat of embarrassment burning her cheeks even as another heat lingered deeper in her body. Her hands waved in the air as she cast about for some satisfactory explanation other than she'd fallen asleep and begun dreaming about *him*.

"I—I'm—how long do you think until we get there?"

"Forty minutes maybe?" he offered casually. "Plenty of time if you want to grab a little shut-eye."

Stiffening, she managed one word. "What?"

"A nap. There's time." Dark lenses shielded his eyes from her scrutiny, but his mouth sat at that casual tilt so typical of him. He looked relaxed. Comfortable. Not at all as if he'd just busted her moaning his name in her sleep. Maybe she'd merely sounded drowsy.

That was it. Because he'd suggested a nap.

Easing down into the soft leather of the seats, she breathed deeply, trying to let go of the tension snapping through her body at the thought she'd given too much away. After a few moments, her limbs relaxed and her eyes drifted closed. And as fatigue overtook her, a low chuckle sounded from across the distance of her consciousness.

"Pleasant dreams, Payton."

Once parked, Payton roused herself from what she only hoped was a quiet sleep and met Nate around the back of the car.

"Warm enough?" he asked, pulling an old blanket from the trunk.

The wind whipped at her hair, but the sun was still bright. Pulling her sweater tight around her, she nodded, peering up at the steep rise of the dunes before them. "I just need to wake up. And if I remember correctly, the hike up'll get my blood pumping."

"Needed that nap, huh?" Nate brushed a thumb beneath her right eye. "Puffy. Cute."

Pulling back, she instinctively raised a hand to check. Puffy? Wonderful.

Clearing his throat, he stretched his arms out, rotating one shoulder and then the other. "Someone must have done a decent job of wearing you out last night."

Only Nate would find a way to turn sleep-swollen eyes into a means of stroking his own ego.

It was a call to trash-talk if ever she heard one. "Not really. Pretty sure I slept through most of it."

He laughed, already making his way up the rise. "You mean you were rendered unconscious. My attentions have been known to overwhelm."

Payton struggled up beside him. "No." Not to be outdone, she feigned a weary sigh. "I drift off when I'm bored." Then fighting a gloating snicker, she added, "Can't say for sure—I barely remember."

She'd take that point.

Yes, sir.

With a swish of her hips and spring in her step, she pushed up the sandy incline, oblivious to Nate's narrowing eyes or the calculating set to his jaw. In a motion too fast to defend against, he reached for her, one powerful arm pulling her into his chest while the other caught her knee to his hip.

Her breath was gone, her mouth agape. All misconceptions about scoring points swept away by the feral gleam in the blue eyes above her.

Straining for air, she gasped, "What are you doing?"

"Reminding you." The gruff threat was her only warning before his lips descended in a brutal crush. The hand at her back snaked up to wind in the mass of her hair and pull her head back, opening her to the thrust of his tongue. Once. Twice. And her body was alive, pulsing with the need for more—

Except it was over and firm hands were setting her a step away.

A single brow rose in question, the seductive threat radiating off him in waves. "Now what were you saying about last night?"

Too stunned to even contemplate a quick-witted barb or smart-mouthed response, she gave him what he demanded. The truth. "It was incredible, and I'll never forget it."

"Good." He winked, sweeping up the discarded blanket with one hand as he started up again. "No more reminders necessary."

Payton stared in shocked disbelief at Nate's retreating form, her indignation on the rise. "I thought we said one night!"

"We did," he called back, barely bothering to turn his head

to respond. "But if one night's all I get, then, babe, you better believe I'm going to make sure you remember it."

By the time they'd skidded down the beach side of the dune, Payton had her outrage, heart-rate and unwilling smile under control. The kiss had completely blindsided her, serving as an effective warning about going for the last word with a man whose drive to win apparently knew no limits of decency. But it also relieved her anxiety about Nate's ability to handle the lovers-to-friends transition.

That was the kiss of a man unconcerned about his ability to turn it on or off. Which suited Payton fine. After so many years of watching every word, she didn't want to censor herself now.

As they hit the damp packed sand, Nate offered a spot beneath his arm. She stepped into the warmth of his hold and they walked in companionable silence.

Gulls soared overhead, and children sprinted through the sand in the distance.

Nate pulled off his glasses and, tucking them into the V of his sweater, turned to her. The normal vibrancy of his eyes had gone brittle beneath the strain of his burden. She knew what was coming. An explanation for this cloak and dagger game with the press, the pretend affair that all too briefly turned real. He didn't want to talk about it, but he would.

"One of the women I dated last year came to me pregnant."

Her heart stalled in her chest as she imagined a child, a golden-haired, blue-eyed bit of Nate, new to the world. And a woman she couldn't even fathom? "My God, Nate…"

What could she say? Congratulations? It hardly seemed as though joyous celebration were the theme of his disclosure considering the lengths to which he was going to shake the press off the scent of his secret. And yet, offering her sympathy seemed equally inappropriate. Questions rose fast and urgent within her, each more desperate to claw free than the one before, but she willed herself silent, waiting for him to go on.

"I was fairly sure she'd been with someone else after we'd ended things, but the timing she described... It was possible. She wanted to get married. Swore up and down the baby was mine. Only, I knew it wasn't. Hell, I suspected." He let out a heavy sigh, ducked and scooped up a handful of sand. Let the grains sift through his fingers. "Maybe I just wished."

Eyes to the darkening waters of Lake Michigan, he straightened. "Whatever the case, I wouldn't marry her. Not until I had a blood test to confirm her claim. She kept pushing. Didn't want her child born a bastard. Didn't want the risk of a prebirth DNA sample." He shook his head, his jaw set off to one side.

Payton waited, her heart in her throat. Her mind blanked beyond anything but the words coming painfully from Nate's mouth.

"In the end, she was born healthy. Not mine. Not that I'd had much doubt at that point."

"Nate, I'm so sorry. That must have been terrible to wait through."

He cast her a quick smile. "Yeah, well. It's been a tough six months. And honestly, the last thing I need is to have the press getting things stirred up again."

She could only imagine what it had been like for him. Of course he didn't want the gory details rehashed for public consumption.

But what she couldn't understand was how a woman who'd actually dated Nate would ever think she'd get away with a ploy like that. "What happened to them?"

"They live in a small town outside of Stuttgart. They're both doing well."

"You keep track of them?"

"Annegret needed help." His tone didn't convey pity, pain or any other depth of feeling. It was matter-of-fact as he stared out over the turbulent waters. "I don't like what happened. Honestly, I don't like her. But she didn't know how to take care of herself. Her father cut her off. The baby's father was married. And I'd been a part of the picture recently enough..." He let out a heavy sigh. "She was desperate and thought she'd found a solution through me."

Perhaps not so ruthless after all...and maybe that was what he didn't want broadcast around the globe.

"I found her a small house. I cover her bills. But the arrangement is she can't talk. If she tries to profit from this in any way, the funding is off. So there's a reason I don't want the press getting a hold of her."

She could see that quite clearly. He'd financed the woman who tried to trap him into marriage with a false paternity claim. It was a risky precedent to set. So why had he done it?

Slanting a glance his way, she asked, "Did you love her?"

Nate's head snapped around, the strangest expression of shock on his face. "No. No, I didn't."

"But you set her up?"

He waved her off. "She was without resources."

"So are a lot of women. Do you have a charitable foundation in place to help them all?" Though, now that she thought about it, he'd tried to do the very same thing with her that afternoon. Was it some kind of white-knight syndrome or was Nate simply the kind of man who couldn't sit idly by when he was capable of making a difference?

"There was a part of me that wouldn't let myself hate her. I knew on some level it was possible the child was mine. And if it turned out to be true, that baby couldn't be born to a father who loathed her. Do you see what I'm saying?"

Payton didn't trust herself to speak. Didn't trust herself to touch him for fear she wouldn't be able to stop. He'd developed an attachment to a child he hadn't believed was his. Forced himself to care—maybe even to love—on the chance it was.

Pushing beyond her own heartbreak, she reached for his hand. "When you found out?"

His head tilted back, eyes fixing on the sky. "I care about Bella. But I can't drop in and out of her life or be her daddy just because she doesn't have one. It would never work with her mother. So I made sure she was taken care of and I let her go."

That kind of emotional toll was unfathomable.

He seemed to have followed her train of thought. "I'd never planned on having a family. I didn't want one thrust upon me. So in that regard it was a relief."

"Because if she'd been yours?"

He met her gaze, steady and unwavering. "I would have married her mother and played the hand life dealt me."

A nervous alarm sounded deep within her. It had been too close. He would have given everything up and she never would have had him back in her life. "Even though you didn't love her?"

"It wouldn't have mattered. If Bella was mine, I would have made us a family. I would have made it work. No issue. But that's the only way I'd make a trek down the aisle."

It wasn't the first time he'd said he didn't want to marry. Though this time she sensed more distaste behind his words. "Pretty adamant about that, huh?"

Nate caught her sidelong glance. "Yeah."

"Was it always like that with you?" She never would have guessed it from the way he'd been in high school; of course, she wouldn't have wanted to see something that didn't support her fantasy that someday he'd marry her!

"I didn't think a lot about it, but probably. My parents' marriage—" He shook his head, squinting off into the distance before letting the rest drop as though it didn't merit voicing. "In college and after, I was working so hard there wasn't time for much more than a quick— There wasn't time for anything involved."

He caught himself in time, though the crinkling around his eyes and a tilt to his lips told her it had been a close thing.

"So kind of you to look out for my delicate sensibilities," she teased.

"Don't be disappointed. I'll slip up another time. Anyway, the romance thing didn't really become an issue until I'd started making a name for myself. And suddenly I couldn't buy a woman a drink without some jerk sticking a mic in my face to ask when the wedding was. It bugged the hell out of me."

She remembered what it was like when his name hit the papers. The constant speculation about how long he'd be able to dodge the gold band. Nate was so good-looking. So charming and charismatic. His success and wealth growing exponentially, it seemed. The press was forever trying to marry him off, practically placing bets as each new female graced his arm.

"I'm sure your dates loved that. It must have been very awkward." It certainly had been when she and Clint faced similar speculation.

"Some of them got the wrong idea." He laughed at the sky and then turned a wry smile on her. "Some had the wrong idea from the start. Honestly, that kind of constant speculation…" He let out a grunt. "It's not like I had a mind for love and marriage before all that, so it didn't take much to turn me off completely."

"But…the right girl?"

"Payton, there are a million 'right' girls. Right for right now. But it doesn't last with me."

"And you still would have married Annegret? You could have lived like that?" She shook her head, fighting the urge to press her hand against the center of his chest. "Without love?"

Nate let out a short laugh. "It's called responsibility. It's not always fun. But it's necessary. Besides, I've lived without falling in 'love' this long," he said, making the taboo emotion sound like something toxic. "I don't want it."

That much was clear. Even so, she couldn't help but wonder… How many women before her had inadvertently given Nate Evans their heart? And had any of them gotten it back?

CHAPTER NINE

THE temperature had dropped with the afternoon sun, and Nate stood at the rear of his car shaking out the sand from the blanket while Payton sat bundled in the front seat. The roof was up and the heater on. Still, she was chilled and he'd wrapped her into a spare fleece he kept in the trunk. She'd looked fragile tucked into the expanse of his oversized pullover. Like something to shelter. Take into his arms and hold.

Which was nuts. Closing the trunk, he rounded to the driver's side door and levered into his seat.

Payton smiled over at him, then nodded back at the darkening sky. "Beautiful, isn't it?"

Her curls were wild with wind-blown abandon. Her cheeks alive with the pink flush of exertion. "Yes. Breathtaking."

Her gaze dropped to her lap, to where only the tips of her fingers peeked from the ends of cuffed sleeves. A sure sign of the nerves he really shouldn't take such satisfaction in stirring.

"Thank you for bringing me out here."

"It was my pleasure. Been a long time since I was here myself. I guess being around you's making me sort of nostalgic."

She smiled, still not meeting his eyes. "Me, too."

The parking lot was deserted. The interior of the car cozy

and intimate. He didn't want to admit just how nostalgic he'd become for things from his high-school past—like long wet kisses and getting naked in the back seat by the beach. Didn't want to admit even to himself how tempting the idea of slipping his fingers into those soft curls and pulling her over him had become.

But making out was a bad idea, and for more reasons than he was six foot five and this was a stick shift convertible with a back seat too small to accommodate a dog. Payton wasn't the kind of woman Nate normally dated. His relationships were short-term and emotionally barren—the women he indulged in them with all too quickly forgotten. And while the sex from the night before had definitely been of the no-strings variety, Payton would never go for something so shallow on an ongoing basis. Hell, he wouldn't want her to. One night, sure. There'd been an attraction and they both understood the parameters, but that kind of mutual attraction would be dangerous to exploit. He couldn't give her serious and she didn't deserve anything less.

And what was more, she was right about there being friendship between them. A bond unique to her. Something he'd missed over the years without exactly understanding why. But now that they had it back, he wouldn't take it lightly.

And Payton was of a similar mind.

Mostly.

He'd seen the way her gaze drifted to his mouth periodically throughout the day. And he'd seen the way she wrenched it away. The quick shake of her head and even quicker redirect to topics of a non-sexually charged nature. She was on board with the plan. The friends plan.

And yet, even knowing sex wasn't how he wanted the relationship to go, the dark fringe of her lashes, the pout of her bottom lip, even the way her bare feet were tucked beneath her—all of those details had somehow slipped under his skin, calling to a part of him that wasn't platonic.

Maybe it was the environment. He'd brought dates here a time or two. Set up a tent and lost himself in their willing bodies.

Only he wasn't thinking about the dates whose names he could barely remember. He was thinking about Payton. About the sound of her sigh at his ear as he pushed inside her. The clutch of her fingers in his hair as he took her against the wall. The way she cried out when he gave her his mouth—

Not where his mind ought to be going.

Not when Payton had felt his gaze on her and turned those soft brown eyes to meet his. Not when the music of the crashing surf was playing for them and the just-one-night they'd agreed to in a moment of more defined clarity than this had come and gone.

Damn it. Until Payton, friendship and sex had always been mutually exclusive. There'd never been a blurring of the line between the two, so he didn't have any experience with the complication she presented now.

Nate gave himself a firm mental shake. One thing he did know. Friends used their mouths for *talking*. So, fingers wrapped around the steering wheel, he forced his gaze to the road and talked. "Tuesday, the charity event."

Payton shifted around until her knees tucked up and her back half pressed against the passenger door. "We'll arrive separately. Maintain a decent distance throughout."

"Though you find it impossible to keep your eyes off me," he amended, just for kicks.

She snickered. "Is that so?"

"Absolutely. I'm temptation incarnate," he answered, heading for the highway, doing his best to ignore the temptation he wanted no part of in the seat beside him.

* * *

By the time they arrived back at Payton's apartment the tension that filled the car when they'd once again found themselves in close proximity had dissipated. They'd made their plans for Tuesday night and fallen into an easy discussion for the remainder of the ride.

Laughing, talking, catching up on the years that had passed them by.

Nate was interested in her teaching. In her plans. Curious about how she'd gotten into the field of special education and not the least bit concerned about the pay or prestige of the school. He simply made her feel good about her choices and, being the only one, it made all the difference.

She unbuckled as he jogged around the car. A steady rain had begun to fall, and though she'd been more than willing to dash into her apartment alone, Nate wouldn't have it.

So without benefit of umbrella, he let her out and ran up the walk beside her.

Rushing to the security door, she tried the key, fumbled and tried again, giving into a frustrated growl as her clumsiness got the both of them a soak. The chill that settled in at the beach was back in full force, making her fingers stiff and useless.

"Here, let me." A warm hand closed around hers and the blanket of wide male torso covered her back as he created a haven for her with his body.

He felt good. Strong and right. Close. Hot.

Oh, God. She'd been so confident. So sure of her ability to handle her emotions where Nate was concerned. *She'd handled them for years!* But now it didn't take more than one touch and her mind and body began their fast descent into bedroom territory. *Wall* territory.

Of course, what she'd been handling ten years ago had been the infatuation of a high-school girl—passionate and dramatic, yes, but ultimately only as deep as the girl herself. Which, at sixteen...

And then there was the little matter of ignorance versus experience. Now that she'd spent a night in his arms, she knew exactly what there was to miss. The heat of his hands, the taste of his skin, the touch of his mouth. Knowing he was more than she'd ever fantasized he would be.

The lock tumbled and Nate pushed the door open and then, following her into the relative warmth of the stairwell, he rubbed her shoulders in a few rough strokes.

"You're soaked."

"Me? What about you?" Rainwater beaded across the light cashmere covering his shoulders and back. Darkened the gold of his hair, weighing it down against his brow to give him a sort of Superman curl that begged to be twisted around her finger.

He waved her off with one hand, taking her elbow in the other. "Let's get you upstairs before you freeze."

Payton stalled. "I can manage. You should get home, though."

Nate's lips curved into a wry twist. "I'll walk you up. Security, remember?"

She did remember. Only the last thing she wanted was Nate back in her apartment. They'd had an incredible afternoon together, but the underlying sizzle of attraction she'd nearly doused had begun to flame again. She didn't want to acknowledge it. Not after the way they'd talked and laughed. She didn't want anything threatening the easy camaraderie.

Still, what could she say? Nate had a way of getting what he wanted. And he wanted to make sure she got into her apartment safely. But he couldn't come in. No matter what. Because if he did, she'd be offering him a drink while he warmed up. Offering to dry his shirt. Offering to help him take if off. Offering everything she had and was. No, he couldn't come in.

She led the way, their quiet tread upon the stairs screaming volumes in the silence. Finally, reaching the landing, she closed her eyes and took a bracing breath. Opened them and turned to Nate. He stood, hands in his pockets, one shoulder propped against the wall.

"Don't worry. I'm not coming in."

"What? I wasn't—"

He shook his head, cutting her off. "Yeah, I think you were."

Her lips parted in protest, but quickly closed again.

He took a deep breath and shifted his weight, glancing down the empty stairwell. "We were together last night, Payton. It's a safe bet we're looking at more than twelve hours to kick whatever residual attraction there is between us back into something safe and platonic. Look, I know what happened between us was different for you. And for what it's worth, it was different for me, too. So maybe we shouldn't worry about a few rogue emotions or whatever we've got going on. If we give it some time the attraction'll die off."

She wanted to believe him. Only she knew from experience that some attractions had staying power for *years*. "What if it doesn't?"

His lips twisted into a wry smile. "Well, then, I guess we'll cross that bridge when we come to it."

She shook her head. She needed this. "I want us to be friends."

"Yeah." He let out a low chuckle as if somehow surprised to find it so. "I do, too. Now get inside before I back you in there myself and ruin this whole buddy-buddy plan we've got going on. I'll see you Tuesday."

CHAPTER TEN

GLASSES clinked, laughter rose and the poignant melody of "Unforgettable" wound around her like a soothing embrace. Inspired by the classic song and its apt description of her past week, Payton swayed with each step on her way to the bar. She could feel the looks. Sense the questions multiplying around her. Heard one woman's sharp, "What?" rise above the din.

She'd been identified—through process of elimination and then conspicuous absence—as Nate's bridesmaid from the back hall, and word had been spreading like whispered wildfire for days. Already she'd faced the most brazen of her social set, descending upon her arrival with horrified expressions and ghastly rumors.

Of course *they* wouldn't believe such nonsense about Payton, but she deserved to know what people were saying...

She responded with the appropriate denials and a flicker of nerves to feed suspicions, then beat a hasty exit, not trusting herself to fight the obnoxious grin threatening to take over her face. Now all she had to do was follow the plan, drop enough subtle hints with Nate to confirm what her reputation was leading people to reject—and Nate's secret would be safe, buried beneath the rubble of Perfect Payton's good-girl reputation.

"What'll you have, miss?"

The bar was stocked with all the top-shelf labels and an

assortment of excellent vintages including a nice Italian white she kept at home. "The Pinot, please."

A glass was in her hand within seconds and, moving to a quiet corner a few feet off, she sipped, her mind bent to the task of fueling the frenzy of gossip already buzzing around her. The wine was cool and refreshing with a hint of fruity sweetness. A perfect complement to the spice of scandal.

Only then a nervous sense of anticipation swirled through her belly, spreading out until it licked over her skin.

Nate.

Lifting her gaze, she found him in an instant, dressed in an immaculately cut white dinner jacket, exchanging greetings with the owner of a bank a few feet from the main entrance. A flash of brilliant blue locked on her, held her rapt, inciting a sudden panic at the betraying heat flaring to life from one look alone.

She stood arrested beneath Nate's considering scrutiny until a feral gleam lit his eyes and the corner of his mouth curved into a dark smile that touched her from clear across the room. Made her shudder.

Not platonic. Not by a long shot. But not for the crowd or the press or protecting a secret either.

What a mess.

She *needed* his friendship. Was desperate for it. But the pull of this attraction between them was playing with her body and mind, and it hadn't died off in the slightest.

To go on as friends after a single night together was one thing, but if that single night turned into a string of nights, a week, a month—something finite, because she knew without question Nate wasn't interested in forever—what would she be left with when it was done?

The press having a field day splashing her face across the rags. Speculating on why she couldn't hold a man like him. Comparing her to whatever bit of glitz he picked up next.

Dredging up Clint and then demanding to know what she'd been thinking.

Who was she kidding?

That was exactly what she'd signed on for the moment she'd given into Nate's kiss, agreeing to go along with the pretense of this affair. Only in the original scenario, she'd have known in her heart it was all a farce. And as it stood now, she was looking at certain heartbreak… *If she gave in.*

Her eyes closed as the weight of the moment settled around her.

Nate wanted her. She wanted friendship.

She didn't stand a chance. Because deep in her heart she wanted way more than that.

Blinking open, she found the tilt to Nate's lips evened, the brilliant blue of his stare gone flat and focused behind her. Her stomach tensed—

"What the hell's going on, Payton?" The question came quiet and accusing from the one person she hadn't considered through all of this.

"Clint." She spun to face him, heat prickling her cheeks as she faced the man she'd nearly married. Tall, with a lean but healthy build, Clint was typically a well-ordered man. Tucked in. Buttoned down. Only this evening, all of that perfection seemed to have slipped the slightest degree. "I didn't know you'd be here tonight. I thought—"

He cut her off with the wave of a hand. "We finished in New York early so I'm back in town." Through with the pleasantries, he glared down at her. "Do you know what people are saying?"

She bristled at his tone of affront and the disapproving glint in his eyes. He had no right. They'd ended the relationship six months before and she knew for a fact he hadn't been sitting home alone that whole time. "People are always saying something. It doesn't matter."

"It matters to me, Payton. What they say about *you* definitely matters to me."

More to the point, it *reflected* on him. That was what this was about. What everything was about.

His hands went to his jacket, where he adjusted the hang, checked the button. All the while, his gaze tracked over her head, scanning the room behind her. "What are you even doing with Nate Evans?"

Her fingers tightened around the stem of her glass. "Nate and I are friends."

Clint's eyes narrowed. The lines at his mouth pulling down. "No, you aren't. Brandt hates him, and in the years we've been together I can't remember you exchanging more than a passing hello."

She opted to let the answer sit. The seconds ticked past as each waited for the other to back down. It wouldn't be her.

His chin jerked back, his brow furrowed and he reached for her arm. "You can't be serious."

"I'm sorry. I should have called you so you didn't find out this way."

"What are you trying to prove, Payton?" Anger flashed in his eyes as the grip at her elbow tightened; she winced, trying to pull free. "He's a player. A *predator*. The last thing you are to Nate Evans is his friend. Mark my words," he hissed, "you're nothing more than a f—"

Tension snapped through the air and a wall of solid muscle closed in behind her. "That's enough, Clint," Nate cut in, his voice deadly low and serious.

Clint's hand released her, his eyes widening as she rubbed her arm then seeking hers apologetically for the unrecognized force of his hold. Taking a step back, he smoothed his jacket as a flush of pink tinged his cheekbones.

"Evans, this is a matter I need to settle with Payton. I'd appreciate it if you gave us a few minutes."

Nate leveled him with an unyielding stare, pulling Payton into his side. "No."

Clint seemed to gauge the moment, notice the growing attention surrounding them, and shook his head. "Payton, this is a mistake."

If she gave in, he would be right. Her heart would pay for her body's wants. But regardless of her personal indecision, publicly she was committed. "It's my mistake to make."

He held her stare a moment. His features hardening as he acknowledged with a terse nod.

And then he was gone. Retreating through the crowd, offering arm claps and boisterous laughter by way of damage control as he went. Stopping for only one furtive glance back.

"You okay?" Nate asked, a single vein throbbing in his neck as he ran his big hands gently over the place where Clint had bruised her.

Payton placed her palm at the center of his chest, felt the violent punch of his heart beneath. The tight rein on his fury as he fought for control. "I'm fine. Clint wouldn't hurt me."

She took a deep breath as Nate's arm crossed her back, his hand settling possessively at the flare of her hip. It was obvious and so good and not at all what they'd discussed. "I thought the plan was to keep some distance. Play hard to get with the press?"

Nate peered down at her tucked beneath his arm. Wide brown eyes met his and he felt the pull of them straight through the center of his body. A little too far north of his belt for his comfort, truth be told, but it was there nonetheless. "The plan changed."

Yeah, like the second that jerk touched her. But in all honesty, things were pretty shaky before that. "Clint just gave us the perfect opportunity to bring this to a head… Tell me to get the hell away from you."

She jerked out of his hold. "You're pretend breaking up with me?"

As furious as Clint had made him, he couldn't help but smile at the indignation in her expression and tone. "No, princess. I'm not pretend breaking up with you. To the contrary, we're going to have our first public spat. And then I'm hauling you out of here to pretend make up with you."

The corner of her mouth twitched with the amusement overtaking the tension of a moment ago. "What exactly is involved in pretending to make up?"

He leaned that much closer, absorbing the rising heat from her skin. "Tell me to walk away and you'll find out." Her eyes widened, pooling dark at his proximity. Giving into the pull of her so close, Nate brushed his knuckles across her shoulder, over the tiny strap of her black dress. "Tell me to keep my hands to myself before someone realizes what's going on."

Her arms crossed as she gave him her shoulder and spoke toward the crowd using one of those hushed tones that sounded convincing but still managed to carry. "You need to stop. Walk away, Nate."

"Do I?" He let out a gruff laugh followed by a deep sigh, close enough to her ear to stir the fine hairs around it. "Why?"

She shivered. "Someone will notice."

It was exactly what was happening. More eyes turned their way with every passing second. "Mmm, notice how close I'm standing? How long we've been talking? The rapid rise and fall of your chest? Your heightened color suggesting an escalated pulse? Are they going to notice that I want you… or that you want me?"

She spun back to him, face flushed, lips parted with a frustrated plea that flickered between hostility and desire. "Nate…"

He caught her chin in his palm, lowering his face to within an inch of hers. "Let them see. I'm done playing games."

Turning her cheek into his hand, she peered up at him and countered, "You never stop playing games."

CHAPTER ELEVEN

WRAPPED in Nate's dinner jacket, Payton stood before the vast expanse of glass staring out at the light bright cityscape surrounding the penthouse apartment. Waiting.

They'd left the event together, fingers twined, allowing a photographer the opportunity to snap a picture as they darted for the car, knowing a counterpart would be staked out at Nate's building as well. Her heart had been racing, her stomach in tumult as she'd waited for him to make his move. But as the scenery blurred past the windows, Nate kept his distance, content to discuss the success of the night. He was confident there'd be a stack of messages from reporters the next morning looking for the scoop on the relationship with Payton Liss. She'd nodded and agreed, all the while contemplating the two roads before her. One smart. One reckless. One right. One wrong. There shouldn't have been any question at all. Only as she'd watched Nate fall into that wide-legged, masculine sprawl, one arm draped across the leather seatback, all she could think was how tempting it would be to climb into his lap. Run her lips across the faint scrub of his jaw. His neck. His mouth…

Now they were back at his apartment, Nate stepped into the reflection in the dark glass as his hands settled over the slope of her shoulders. "What are you thinking?"

That she was crazy and he was dangerous, and if she wasn't

very careful she'd end up exactly where she wanted to be. "That your secret's safe."

"I think it is. In large part thanks to Clint."

She stiffened. Looked past his image into the night where streetlights illuminated spots of scenery and the red streaks of taillights disappeared around the corner two blocks down. "I should have thought about how he'd react. Warned him. But I didn't think of him at all."

He squeezed gently over her muscles, drawing the tension out with slow strokes. "He's jealous." Not a question. "Wants you back."

"Maybe. Yes." At least he thought he did. Clint wanted the woman she'd pretended to be.

"Not quite the idiot I thought, then. But you don't want him, do you?"

She shook her head. "No. I really don't."

"Good." His breath came close to her ear. "Then that's out of the way."

A warning skittered over her skin and she turned out of his hold. Stepped back. Swallowed. "I should go. Tomorrow's a school day. We both have to work."

Nate dismissed her protest with a flick of his hand. Nonsense. Inconsequential.

"I wouldn't stop you if marrying Clint was what you wanted." His gaze drifted to her mouth, to where she'd anxiously set her teeth into her lip. "Or maybe I would."

He was flirting, playing as he always did.

Yeah, sure he was.

A nervous laugh escaped her and he took a step forward, one golden brow arched in question. "You think I wouldn't?"

Okay, this was it. Her chance to talk sense. She shook her head and took another step back. Slowly. She wouldn't stand a chance if this turned into a game of chase. "You might be cutthroat and relentless and everything else they say about you, but you're also honest and honorable. You've been that way your whole life—it's just not quite as obvious the way the papers paint you now."

"You're a Pollyanna," he countered with that mischievous glint in his eyes. "But I like it. Did I mention I had a bridge to sell you?"

"No way, Nate," she scoffed, her confidence returning with their banter. "You do the right thing. I trust you. It's why you— your friendship means so much to me." One of the reasons anyway.

He took another step forward. "I'm glad to hear honesty is important to you, because about that friendship thing—"

"Stop." Before it was too late and she ended up losing everything because she couldn't resist the sound of his voice and lure of his words. "Let's think about this for a minute."

"I've already thought about it," he answered flatly.

"Listen," she pleaded. "Imagine we have two roads before us. Friendship is like an interstate highway."

Nate's chin pulled back, amusement battling with distaste. "Remind me not to hire you for any marketing jobs."

Ignoring the little boy who didn't want anyone to make the rules but him, she went on. "The highway is long and constant. Scenic. Pleasant. We could travel it for years."

Arms crossed, he nodded once. "Right."

"Sex is like a blind path through a lush jungle." At his slow-spreading grin, she cleared her throat and stared at her shoes. "Sure, it's hot and wet and exciting—"

"You're trying to talk me out of this?"

"—right up to where the ground falls away in a sheer drop and all the fun is over." And her heart lay a hundred feet below, battered and crushed on some rocky riverbank.

"So what you're saying is…you've got some kind of Tarzan fantasy you want to act out."

The corners of her mouth twitched even as she tried to glower at him. "Nate!"

Unrepentant, he went on. "Because I've got one of those rainforest shower things in my bathroom. You could wear a ratty bikini with a few strategically placed rips. I'll wear a shredded shirt and cargo shorts."

She scrunched her eyes, trying hard not to let her imagination follow where his dirty mouth led…

"I'll invite you back to my room. Show off my *vine*."

She burst out laughing, the tension that threatened to overwhelm her dissipating under Nate's juvenile antics.

He was joking. Well over the line of ridiculous—so why was she suddenly burning with the need to touch him? Tear the sleeves off his shirt and make him beat his chest and roar.

Darn it! He was working around her defenses. But she had more to fight for than a good time. She needed him. In the few days since they'd reconnected she'd discovered how incredible it was to have someone who really saw her. Let her laugh and joke. Have an opinion that didn't follow everyday convention. Someone to talk with. She didn't want to give it up. Couldn't go back to the lonely isolation that had been so much a part of her life for too many years now. It didn't matter the number of people surrounding her, there was only one who actually saw her.

"Nate, this is serious." Her lips pressed together in a firm line as she sought for a means to make him understand. "I don't have a lot of friends—"

"I do. I'll share. And if they aren't enough, we'll start trolling the social clubs together."

"You're making jokes," she shot back. "But the idea of risking something this important isn't funny to me. You pick up pretty, shiny playthings at every turn, have your fun and toss them aside without a backward glance once you've lost interest. I don't want to be another discarded toy in your wake."

A muscle in Nate's jaw ticked, his posture taking a subtle shift. "It wouldn't be like that."

"No? Why not? Is the press really so far off in what they say about you?"

"I don't know, Payton, how accurate are they about you? Could they have predicted it would be like this between us?" He broke off and shoved a hand through his hair. Blew out a harsh breath and then seemed to pull inward for a count. And then he was back in control. Cool. Steady. Reasonable.

"It's not that I *don't want* to be friends, Payton. It's that *I don't think we can be*. Not with what's between us.... I *know* you feel it, too."

She bowed her head with a stubborn shake, hiding the conflict warring in her eyes. Unwilling to reveal the power of his effect on her. How right he was.

She felt it. The connection that messed with her head and threw off her equilibrium, made her dizzy and hot and wanting to justify all kinds of things she knew she shouldn't. Made her want a man more controlling than all the other men in her life put together. Insanity.

"You're going to deny it?" he drawled, low and rough, ominously seductive. The change in tone and tack alerting her to the coming danger.

Clint had been right. Nate was a predator. And she was prey.

She swallowed hard and, shaking her fuddled head, answered, "Yes."

"Hmm. You seem confused. Conflicted." He leaned closer so the heat of him scorched her skin. "I can help with that."

Panic burst to life. Her eyes bulged at her body's betrayal and her own stupidity. He overwhelmed her. Dominated her senses in the realm of desire.

Get it together!

"No." Some rebuke, all breathy and weak.

"Convincing," he taunted, eyes gleaming. "So which is it, Payton? Yes. No. Do you even know yourself?"

"This isn't fair, Nate."

He leveled her with his gaze. "I think it is." Then after a moment that cocky grin broke out across his lips. Trouble. "Here, how's this for fair? We'll put it to a test. I'll kiss you."

Her chin tucked, but he waved off her concern. "Don't worry, in the interest of accuracy, I'll give it my all. And when I'm done, you tell me if you still think we can be friends."

This time her mouth and body worked in unison, her steps carrying her back in quick repetition as her hands flew up to ward him off. "No. That's a very bad idea. You said the attraction would die off. It's only Tuesday. A few days! We haven't given it enough time."

He closed in on her again, confident and sure. Overwhelming in ways beyond his powerful build. "Has it? Only been a few days for you?"

God, that look in his eyes. He knew. A few days plus thirteen years.

This was a disaster. "Nate, we're talking about more than just this next moment—"

"Damn straight we are. I thought I'd proved I could last more than a minute Saturday night."

Suddenly the wall rose up behind her, ending her retreat. Heat burst out over her chest, neck and cheeks. "You know what I mean. I want us to be friends."

His gaze turned serious and for an instant she thought he might walk away, but then he shook his head in response to the hope lighting her eyes. "I do, too, Payton. But it's not going to happen if we can't handle the attraction. Put it in its place."

"We can!" She flicked her hands out in a frantic motion to

sweep him away. "We start by putting some distance between us, that's all, and we'll handle this fine."

But instead of stepping back, Nate braced one hand at the wall above her head and caught her wrist in the other. "You seem so sure. But what happens if we touch…accidentally?"

There was nothing accidental about the stroke of his thumb across the sensitive skin of her wrist or the way he leaned close enough that the air around her went thick and a current of need coursed through her.

His grip was loose, the barricade of his powerful arm limited to one side. She could have pulled away, should have fled, but even when he released his hold to draw the tip of one finger down the length of her neck, the only escape she could manage was to shut her eyes.

"Are you going to go up in flames at the DVD store? Melt all the ice cream in the frozen-food aisle when we hit the market some night?" His breath at her ear sent a jolt through her nervous system, accelerating her pulse and pushing heat to lick at the surface of her skin.

"You know I want you," she whispered on a shaky breath. "But I want something else more."

"Are you sure?"

"Yes." The single word hitched free, begging for something more than what she claimed.

He was so close she could almost feel the light rasp of his jaw, the strength of his body against her, the too-confident smile at his lips. "Then put your money where your mouth is and show me."

"What's a kiss going to prove?" she asked, wanting to kick herself for the husky quality of her question. Only if she dared move her leg an inch, she had no doubt she'd find it wrapped around Nate's hip and all her resistance would be for naught.

Nate straightened, taking the warmth and promise of his body away. "Simple. If we can stop, then we've got a shot at being friends."

It was all too easy to let herself believe the kiss was inevitable. That Nate had decided this was the way to handle the dilemma of their attraction...and so it would be done. But she knew it wasn't true. Somewhere along his line of reasoning the pure masculine scent of him had slipped beneath her skin, making her ache and want. Wonder. Was he right? Was it even possible to have the friendship knowing the fuel of desire burned so hot between them?

Her body trembled. Maybe she had to know, too.

She searched his eyes for understanding, for mercy. "And if we can't stop?"

Nate's features pulled taut, his nostrils flaring with a forced intake of breath. The arm he'd braced against the wall gave at the elbow, slowly bringing him into her space. "Then we don't."

It was one kiss. And all she had to do was stop there. Her gaze fixed on his mouth as memories of what he'd done with it only a few nights before bombarded her.

Her vision hazed. Lips parted.

Simple. As he said. Just stop after one. "Okay. A test."

Bowing his head close, he brushed his lips against her ear so she shivered with delicious chills. "You know what used to drive your brother absolutely *insane*?"

Brandt? The fog of rising lust thinned as she wondered what in the world—and then her breath caught at the memory of a long-ago afternoon. Her brother storming through the door bellowing about his exam—and how Nate Evans *always* blew the curve.

Her eyes flew wide as Nate murmured his final warning. "I test *very* well."

CHAPTER TWELVE

HE COULDN'T just kiss her. Not Nate. No. He had to make a point as he did it. Eyes locked with Payton's—forcing her to watch as he whittled the distance between them, covered her mouth with his and sank into his task with a slow, deliberate pressure. She couldn't close her eyes or look away. But even as panic licked amongst the flames engulfing her, she held strong. Stoically taking what he gave her, she told herself to enjoy it—that it would be the last. If she could maintain her control here, then she'd have had her cake and eaten it, too— one night with Nate and a lifetime of friendship to follow.

She watched him, watching her.

Gentle suction pulled at her restraint. The back and forth rub of firm masculine lips wore at her resolve. God, he was good. Patient and skilled and, if memory served, just getting started. Her pulse skittered faster, a needy ache throbbed low in her belly. Twisting tight.

Be strong.

Even if holding back nearly killed her, no one actually died from denial.

She could do it. She could outlast this one pleasured assault and walk away from the temptation of more. Secure the friendship she didn't want to let go.

Keep Nate forever...

And never again feel the stroke of his tongue skimming the

tight seam of her lips, pushing her molten core past containment, spilling liquid fire through her veins.

Oh, God, she couldn't—shouldn't.

His fingers threaded through the hair at the nape of her neck, wound and pulled with a tension so deliciously forbidden there was nothing to do but open on a trembling gasp. And then he was sliding into her mouth—hot and wet—in a slow, measured thrust and retreat that wiped her mind of anything beyond *more*. Having as much of this kiss as she could for as long as he gave it.

His mouth angled, taking them deeper. Taking more. Taking everything.

She could still stop. Still have the security. Have what they'd had all those years before. Memories rose to fight each decadent thrust of his tongue: Nate with his arm around her as they watched TV on the couch; raking the yard with her; leaning over her shoulder to help with her homework; laughing, with his head back and eyes shut over some dumb joke.

Friendly memories. Warm.

Only there was a constant through each and every one she hadn't wanted to acknowledge until now. As she'd laughed alongside him or taken his assistance with a grateful smile, through it all she'd been fantasizing about—aching for—a moment like the one she resisted now. Where Nate wanted more.

And in that instant she realized if she did the "right thing", took the safe path, she'd be doing exactly what she'd sworn she wouldn't. Living a lie. Pretending to be a friend when she wanted to be a lover. Forcing herself into a mold that didn't fit.

She blinked, once, twice. Gave into the heavy weight of her lids and closed her eyes. Gave up her fight against an inevitable hurt and loss in the future and stopped resisting the want and need that was now.

Her eyes closed and her body went lax in his arms. It was as though she'd simply given up and Nate felt the loss of her fight like a blow to the gut.

He shouldn't care. He never cared. Relationships and whatever came of them were simply what they were. Enjoyable until they weren't. Always on his terms.

But not this time. This time it was out of his control and driving him nuts.

Didn't she understand he couldn't *make* himself see her in a platonic light? It wasn't *choice* firing his blood at the sight of her alone?

Damn, he had to let go, get his head around the fact that he couldn't have her.

His arms loosened their hold. His marauding mouth eased from its plunder as he drew back to break the kiss—the kiss that wouldn't break because the lips he'd poured his every skill and desire into had followed his retreat.

His pulse jacked.

Slight hands balled against his chest, released, crept higher and balled again.

Was he reading this right?

He tried to pull back—to see her face—but those slim arms were wrapped around his neck, clutching and clinging tight as her fragile plea shattered against his lips. "Don't stop."

His breath rushed out on a groan that was relief and desire and victory all in one, and in a combination so potent it nearly took him to his knees. And then she was alive in his arms, opening wide beneath the crush of his kiss, taking everything he gave and demanding more. Meeting the thrust of his tongue with the stroke of her own so they mingled in a sensual dance that was hot and wet and urgent.

Rhythmic. Erotic.

And not nearly enough. Nothing was enough. No matter how he touched her, how she moaned against his lips, pushed and pulled at his clothing until it hung half free of his limbs, begged with quiet sobs as he worked past her panties, teasing one finger and then two through her slippery arousal, it wasn't enough. He had to be inside her. Had to have her. Completely.

His body vibrated with need beyond control. Banding his arms across her back, he lifted her from her feet.

"Say it again," he demanded, his mouth rough against her throat as he moved to the couch.

"Don't stop," she panted, her hands grasping at his shoulders. Her knees settling into the leather at either side of him so her skirt rode up her thighs. Opening her to him.

Damn, he could feel her, soft and hot, through the damp swatch of her silk panties.

Pushing violently at his half-open fly, he freed himself, giving into the temptation of that fragile silk barrier. He palmed her bottom and guided her to the bare skin of his shaft. Had to grip the base of the couch when her hands clenched, her body tensing as she slid against the length of him.

"Don't stop…" she breathed again, her words taking on a desperation that only fed the madness burning within his veins. Her hair hung wild and loose around her face, her breasts swayed half exposed from when they'd wrestled with the straps of her dress. Her eyes were dark, heavy lidded and pleading as she moved over the straining ridge of his erection. "I can't stop."

Too. Much.

Not. Enough.

Reason and restraint snapped. He had her beneath him, her lips parted in a silent cry of pleasure that tore through his very soul as he pushed inside.

Wet friction embraced him. Took hold of his sanity and tossed it aside as he drew back and drove deep again, setting a relentless rhythm of triumph and possession.

He had her. Writhing beneath him. Coming apart around him. The clutch of her slick walls urging him to follow. She felt so good…too good…too good…

Nate froze.

Too good.

She felt too good because he wasn't wearing a condom. Buried inside her, a hair's breadth from release with the receding waves of Payton's orgasm pulsing around him, he didn't dare move.

Control. Where was his control?

His teeth ground together with a series of audible pops as he slowly withdrew. Images of the past six months sliding through his mind, gripping him like icy talons. What the hell was wrong with him?

"Nate?" Her hands smoothed down his chest, her eyes searching. Taunting him with a welcome he couldn't accept. Yet.

"Condom, Payton," he managed on a hoarse growl as he found the foil packet he'd never forgotten before.

"Thank God you remembered." She shook her head, watching him as if he'd managed something remarkable. Well, he'd stopped in time. That was pretty damn remarkable. But the fact that he'd been inside her at all—

Never before. He'd never lost it like that. Never come so close to losing everything.

Never again.

Covering himself, he reached for her. "Now where were we?"

An hour later, they lay sprawled across Nate's bed, naked beneath a blanket of moonlight. Payton traced patterns across his skin, circling this way and that. Her touch was light. Sweetly exploratory. And arousing all too soon after they'd collapsed together mere minutes before.

This was the point where he typically employed some trusty exit or eject strategy, but tonight the foundation of caring and history he had with Payton was throwing him off. Nothing within his arsenal of disentanglement techniques suitably handled the unprecedented situation with a woman whom was both lover and friend and who he had no intention of letting go. At least not any time soon.

Tucking his chin, he watched her fingertips walk the steps of his ribs, climb higher and then smooth across the center of his chest.

Maybe there wasn't anything to handle at all. So long as he used his head and a measure of restraint, no one would get hurt.

Yes, he wanted her. Had nearly lost it when he thought he couldn't have her. But even so, he knew himself—the kind of love that led to marriage and family wasn't part of his makeup, and this wouldn't last forever.

As though reading his mind, Payton turned her eyes, soft and vulnerable, to his. "What are we doing?" she asked quietly. "You didn't want a relationship. You told me. So what is this?" Her question held no accusation, challenge or demand, just a need to know something he didn't have the understanding to explain.

"No, I didn't. But nothing turns out the way I expect with you. I think I know how something's going to play and then suddenly I'm staring open-mouthed at a scenario I couldn't have predicted. This, what's between us—" he shook his head "—it's not common in my life."

"Mine either. But since neither of us seemed able to ignore it, let's just enjoy it for as long as this lasts." She leaned in to kiss him, and he saw the flicker of sadness—remorse maybe—that crept into her eyes. He wanted to make it go away. Only he couldn't lie to her. Promise something they both knew wouldn't happen.

What he could offer was the possibility of a scenario he very much hoped would become reality. He ran a finger along her jaw and tipped her face to his. "You know, just because we're detouring through the jungle now, it doesn't mean there won't be a chance to veer back onto the main drag later."

The fact that it hadn't happened before didn't guarantee it never would. This was Payton, after all, and the power of her optimistic determination knew no bounds.

She blinked up at him, her big brown eyes so wide with trust, once again taking him back through the years to a time when she was the only one who saw the potential in him—to her limitless faith.

He didn't want to let her down. He'd almost done it tonight. Almost let them both down.

"I don't know what's going to happen, Payton, but I'll always care for you."

She nodded, letting her smile spread. "Then how about we forget about what might happen? Let the future take care of itself and, for now, we'll have fun."

She deserved better.

He couldn't give it to her but neither could he let her go. So he shoved the bitter knowledge aside, focusing instead on the now. Payton in his bed. Smiling. Sexy and bare.

CHAPTER THIRTEEN

SATURDAY morning Payton emerged from Nate's bedroom bleary-eyed and desperate for caffeine. Waking alone, she'd managed to locate her panties and Nate's discarded tee shirt from the night before, but after minutes of fruitless searching for her jeans she abandoned the quest. Bare-legged, she padded down the hall following the fresh-brewed scent of dark roast coffee.

They'd been to a wine bar for dinner the night before and, though delicious, that third glass was wreaking havoc on her head this morning. Halfway through their first small plate of chorizo-stuffed dates, a couple of Nate's friends had turned up and joined them bar-side. Not the society crowd Payton was so keen to get away from, just a wonderfully funny and intelligent couple Nate had known for years.

The tone of the evening had been set when Nate introduced her as his girlfriend and she'd choked on her drink and then flushed so red that no one could ignore it. Soon they'd all found themselves laughing about the label, swapping stories about Nate at various ages and overall having such a great time her shaky tolerance was the last thing on her mind.

After, Nate had brought her back to his apartment and proceeded to make love to her until the wee hours of the morning—which invariably had as much to do with the drag in her step as that last glass.

She turned into the kitchen, rubbed a lazy hand at her eye hoping Nate still found 'puffy' cute, and poured some coffee.

Nate's voice sounded from the front room in a low rumble. Probably taking care of some business while she'd been dead to the world in his bed. But noting more rasp than usual, she wondered if perhaps he'd had a glass too many as well. Not likely. Nate didn't get caught up in excess.

She took a steaming swallow, then cradled the mug at her chest to absorb the warmth both inside and out.

"So it's true?" The demand filtered down the hall, sounding almost accusatory, and she considered returning to the bedroom. Maybe taking a shower while he wrapped things up.

Then… "Look, it just sort of happened. We haven't talked since high school, but once we started…you remember what a cool girl she was. Fun, you know?"

She set the mug down on the counter harder than she'd intended, tried to steady it with clumsy hands. This conversation was about *her*. She stepped back to the hall. She definitely shouldn't be listening in.

"Is it serious?" Her brow puckered at the croaked question and she slowed her steps. Visualizing Nate's considering expression. What could he say? It had only been a week since their first night together. And yet they knew each other.

Nate's exasperated sigh propelled her forward. Toward the conversation rather than away from it. She was in the apartment and he was talking about her. Better to let him know she was awake, before this became something uncomfortable between them. Only it wasn't until she turned into the front room and encountered Nate's clear blue eyes—on a face twenty-five years older than the one she went to bed with—that understanding came.

Nate's father. *Mr. Evans*, seemingly paralyzed as he gaped

with what she could only describe as open-mouthed appreciation at the region where her tee shirt ended and bare legs began.

Nate muttered a particularly colorful obscenity, stepping from behind his dad. "Morning, Payton."

Before she could reply, the Evans elder regained use of his faculties, brows slamming down in an all too familiar scowl. He crossed his arms, turning to the younger version of himself, a man who left tycoons cowering, and demanded, "You couldn't tell me she was *here*?"

Nate shrugged—*shrugged!*—and covered his stubbled jaw with one wide hand in a blatant effort to hide his growing smile. "I thought I could get you out before you caught us."

"Uh-uh-umm-I—" She broke off, shaking her head, at a total loss for words as she stumbled back a few steps. Now she understood the dialog she'd overheard, and it was definitely a conversation she didn't want to be a part of.

"Relax, Payton. He's not going to call your mother."

Thanks for that, Nate.

"Why don't you get showered? Dad and I are going to run out and pick up a little breakfast. Wishbone sound good, Dad?"

The older man grunted. "That'll do."

Not for her it wouldn't. "Uh, Nate, I actually need to…" She waved a hand around, casting about for a good excuse to get the heck out of there. Sitting around with Nate's friends was one thing, but Mr. Evans? After he'd given her a B- in World Economics and busted her shacked up with his son? No, thank you. "I need to take care of *that thing* I told you I had to do today."

Mr. Evans wasn't impressed. And Nate simply shook his head with an expression that said, "Fat chance."

"Give me a second with my dad here and I'll be right back."

"Sure," she managed, still on the brink of hyperventilating.

Time to flee. Be gone. Vamoose!

She'd finally tasted the mortification of being caught in a compromising position—something most people probably experienced back in high school—and she had no idea how she would survive it.

Nothing could be worse.

Desperate to make her exit, she hastily spun away—square into the jutting leg of the sideboard. Pain shot through her foot as she tripped forward with a sharp cry.

Sadly, not enough pain to block the two voices following in quick report.

"Oh, God in heaven."

"Dad, turn around!" Nate begged, laughter lacing his plea.

Her eyes bugged and then pinched shut as her crouched position and the cool breeze across her backside registered. She grabbed for the hem of the tee shirt, tugging it down to cover the bit of hot pink lace she'd picked up to entertain Nate.

A peek out of one squinched eye at both Evans men doubled over ensured they were highly entertained. "This is not funny!"

At least his father had the good grace to look away, but Nate simply straightened, hands on his hips, his gaze fixed on her butt. "Oh, Payton. I'm sorry, honey, but yes it is." Then ducking low, he wrapped an arm around her and pulled her up and against him. "Is your foot okay?" he asked, one palm warming her hip.

She looked at her second and third toes, both red and throbbing angrily, and sighed. "Just stubbed. I'm fine." Really it was her pride suffering more than anything else right then.

Nate glanced back over his shoulder. "Close your eyes, old

man, or I'm putting you in a home. You've had enough cheap thrills for one morning."

A dismissive, "Yeah, yeah," came from behind them, and with that she was swept up into the cradle of Nate's arms for the princess-style escort back to his room. Too bad her scantily clad bum was hanging out, ruining the effect.

When Nate deposited her at the door to the master bath, she touched his arm and looked up at him imploringly. "Uh, Nate, how about I let you catch up with your dad? I'll see you—"

His hand closed over hers with a telling squeeze. "No. I'm giving you thirty minutes and then you'll sit there with us enjoying breakfast and making small talk. That's what good *girlfriends* do."

"Are you afraid of your dad?" She raised a mocking brow and met one in return.

"Aren't you?"

"Well, yes." Everyone had been. He'd been the toughest teacher at school. "But he's *your* dad."

"Yeah, who drove all the way into the city to slap a paper with our picture in it against the side of my head."

The image that conjured had her near giggles, only what was behind it wasn't very funny. "He seems upset."

Acknowledging with the barest nod, Nate extracted the weapon in question from where he'd tucked it under his arm and flipped through until he found their page. "Here we go."

Setting it on the granite countertop, he leaned close so the heat of his chest warmed her back as they read. Payton's brows drew down as she scanned the column. There was more information than she would have expected them to find. Particularly since she'd been ignoring the reporters' calls herself.

"Did you do this?" she asked.

"Some." He pointed to the line about being seen around town since the relationship had been publicly outed earlier that week. "I had my assistant Deborah drop the hint that we'd been keeping it under wraps. Hey, they hit the school where you work, too."

An involuntary groan slipped out and Nate chuckled above her. "What, it can't be the first time the press showed up there."

"No. Not the first time." There'd been a few months following her father's death where the interest in her had peaked and reporters seemed to lurk around every corner, waiting for the opportunity to pump her fellow teachers for information.

How was she holding up? Was a wedding in the works? Could the romance sustain through the tragedy? Would she be leaving the school to take a seat at Liss Industries?

It hadn't won her any friends at the new school back then, but over the past year the alienation she'd experienced had died down along with the press's interest. Still, every time she'd found herself pictured in the paper she'd sensed a subtle backlash. She wasn't looking forward to the reaction come Monday.

"It's pretty much what I'd expected." Nate knocked the paper aside with a knuckled fist and stepped back. "Deborah's got a few more nuggets to dole out over the next weeks, so I'd say we're in good shape."

"Mission accomplished."

Rubbing a wide palm over the scrub of his jaw, he nodded. "As for my dad—I don't really talk to him about the women I'm dating, but I should have told him about us. Things are different with you."

"Different?" Hope lit through her veins, pushing into her heart with welcoming ease.

"Yeah." He met her with a blind stare. "He knows you. Probably feels as protective of you from those high-school days as I do."

Nate shook his head, thankfully too wrapped up in the

situation with his father to notice the falter of her smile as her most vital organ hollowed out. It was stupid. She knew what she'd signed on for and the surest way to ruin it or any chance of maintaining a friendship after would be to spend every minute they were together imagining more meaning into Nate's words than they deserved.

"I'm a big girl," she said, as much a reminder to herself as to him. "He doesn't need to worry about me."

This brought a low chuckle as his gaze raked down the length of her. "Okay, *big girl*. You were all over this whole girlfriend business last night. Rolling around in the title like you owned it. Time to start paying those dues."

She let out a cough. "Dues? Come on—"

"Payton, I'm not asking you to see him through his retirement years." He raked a hand through the thick mess of sandy blond spikes. "Just to hang out for an hour or two and show my dad I'm not treating you like some floozy or pulling the wool over your poor innocent eyes."

And suddenly she realized he was serious. "You're worried about what he thinks."

"That surprises you?"

It shouldn't have. But after having spent a lifetime worrying—obsessing—about how her every action would be interpreted by her own father, she'd never really thought of Nate, who always came across so fun and carefree, as having the same issues. "I guess you never seemed…concerned."

"Yeah, well, my mom took off when I was young, so it was just my dad and me. And, you know him, he's not a halfway kind of guy. Since raising me fell wholly on his shoulders, he took the job seriously. Made a lot of sacrifices and spent a lot of years making sure I knew right from wrong, worked hard and did the right thing. Honestly, he couldn't care less about the financial kudos or bank account I've built. He measures my success—and his—by the kind of man I've made. So, yes. It matters to me that he knows he did a good job."

Her heart rolled over with a little sigh for this man who loved his father and had his priorities so well aligned. If only there were room in his heart for more. "He did a very good job. Go get me some grub while I get dressed and I'll tell him so."

It was early afternoon by the time they'd said their good-byes and the elevator doors slid shut with a quiet whoosh. Nate leaned a shoulder against the brushed-steel interior and watched his father. Waiting.

Payton had recovered from her initial embarrassment by the time they'd returned with breakfast. He'd expected the quiet poise and well-mannered reserve she was known for, but she'd been relaxed and comfortable, charming his old man with her bright smile and fresh take on the adventures of academia.

She'd been perfect. Too perfect. Too comfortable. Too right a fit between what had always been just the two of them. God only knew what his dad was thinking now—but he didn't have long to wait to find out.

Solemn eyes that had been shining with merriment half an hour before turned on him. "What are you doing with her?"

Or, more to the point, what was a nice girl like Payton Liss doing with a guy like him? "We're just having some fun, Dad. It's not serious so don't start knitting any booties."

A beat of silence and then, "Does she know that?"

Staring at the numbers as each floor illuminated and went dark, he offered a single nod. "Give me some credit. We wouldn't have gotten anywhere near a bed if she didn't."

"She's not like the others."

Nate fought back a grin. His father hadn't had a say in his sex life since he'd slapped a box of condoms in his hand in high school and sat him down for a man-to-man. "What do you know about the others?"

"I know you haven't introduced me to a date since you were seventeen."

"You already knew Payton. And it wasn't like I brought her home for dinner. She walked in before I could get rid of you."

His dad let out a derisive snort. "I know you're linked to one woman after another, but it never lasts more than a couple weeks because there's no connection."

Yeah, he supposed if anyone had the skill set to recognize something like that it was his dad. Hindsight and all. "You've been spending too much time with your nose in the tabloids."

"I saw you laughing with her. The way she looked at you." His dad stared him straight in the eye. "This one's not going to let go so easily."

Nate shook his head. "Yes, she will."

When the time came, she'd have to. And until then, she wouldn't get too close.

He wouldn't let her.

CHAPTER FOURTEEN

THEY'D spent the evening enjoying dinner, drinks, and non-stop laughter at the Gold Coast home of Diane and Garry Ortiz. Nate tried to warn her ahead of time about his former Marketing VP's larger-than-life personality trapped in a pixie-sized body—but it wasn't until Payton found herself gasping for breath within the enthusiastic squeeze of Diane's shockingly strong arms that she fully grasped his meaning. Stunned, she took a step back, laughing as Nate steadied her with a hand at her hip.

"Diane, I think you broke my date," he joked, dodging to avoid the swat of her arm.

"Oh, stuff it, Nate." She took a deep breath that seemed to fill her entire body, nearly bringing her to her toes, and then let it out in a huge rush. "It's just so wonderful to have finally met you, Payton. I can't believe the nerve of this guy in keeping you a secret for so long."

"Thank you. Tonight was so much fun."

Diane cast a mocking scowl Nate's way. "See? She likes us. No reason to keep her holed up the way you did."

It was hardly the case. As absurd as the suggestion had been, Nate hadn't been kidding about sharing his friends. In their few short weeks together, he'd been steadily circulating her through the various groups he socialized with, encouraging relationships outside himself. Keeping up his end of the bargain while maintaining the ruse around the timing of their reunion for the sake of a child half a world away.

Cocking his signature grin, he winked. "Guess I just wanted her all to myself."

Diane waved him off, pulling Payton into another suffocating embrace, and then set her back with a satisfied smile. "About time you found one worth hanging onto, Evans."

"Definitely." He looked casual, utterly at ease with the implication they had a future together. But Payton knew the truth.

With Nate romancing her several nights a week, filling her days with unexpected surprises, texts and phone calls—it should have been heaven. But their romance was running on borrowed time.

Nate had ways of reminding her. Nothing overt or hostile. Just a subtle distancing when he sensed she was getting ahead of herself. The problem was, she didn't want the distance or to hold back, and more than that she didn't want Nate holding back either. What they had wasn't going to last and, no matter how she sliced it, when the romance ended her heart would break. There was no defense against it. So until that happened, she was going after everything she could get.

Sunshine poured clear and bright from the October sky, the lingering Indian summer giving the city as a whole a reason to smile. Payton, clipping down the sidewalk in her favorite flowing skirt and calf-hugging, heeled leather boots, was no exception. It was an off day from seeing Nate, and thanks to a field trip her afternoon classes were cancelled—which left her free to catch up on a few overdue errands. Only as she rounded the corner of her block, she caught sight of Nate—dangerously appealing in Aviators and dark jeans—pushing off the rough brick pillar at the end of her walk.

"What are you doing here?" she called, rushing forward. "I thought you had meetings all afternoon?"

"Being the boss has its benefits." Nate stretched out his arms, gesturing around him. "Too nice a day to be cooped up indoors. Let's drop your stuff and take a ride."

Payton frowned down the street. "I'd love to, but I've made appointments around town. Papers to sign at the lawyers. Stuff I've been putting off too long."

Nate slipped his fingers beneath the lapels of her jacket and tugged her gently into him, his cajoling smile running at full strength. "So reschedule. Lawyers do it all the time."

"No, I shouldn't—"

"Sure you should."

She sighed, bristling slightly at Nate's domineering attitude. But then he tucked her beneath his jaw and it felt so good in his arms. So right.

"Tell your lawyer it's a crime against nature to waste a day like this one and you'll see him next week." His fingers sifted through the curls at her back, the touch sending a shiver of pleasure skirting her spine.

It would be easy enough to reschedule. But Nate simply expecting she drop everything to accommodate his whim didn't exactly sit right. Even if she had been thinking about him all day, she didn't want to be treated like just another one of his beck-and-call girls.

No, she was making too much of it. The man wanted to see her so he'd dropped by. Big deal. It was a nice thing.

And it wouldn't last forever.

"Come on. We'll play hooky. It'll be fun."

"Hooky?" she scoffed, giving in with a slow caress of her hands down his chest. "What are we going to do? Go to the mall? Catch a movie? Hide out under the bleachers?"

Nate's smile was pure mischief, his tone pure seduction. "Is that what you did?"

"Please. Like I've ever ditched."

He'd moved into leering territory now, his blue-eyed gaze running the length of her. "But I bet you wanted to."

"I did," she replied, her answer escaping on a wistful sigh.

"Yeah," he answered, face tilting toward the sky. "Me, too. But I couldn't exactly get away with it when Dad was teaching two doors down from my homeroom."

"I guess not."

"But no one from the office would dare call him now."

She let out a conspiratorial laugh. "And your secret is safe with me."

Grinning, Nate pulled his phone from his pocket and handed it over. "Reschedule."

Five minutes later Nate threw his leg over the black bike parked at the curb, watching with satisfaction as Payton's eyes went wide and her lips parted on a small intake of breath.

He brought the bike off its center stand and held out the spare helmet. "Hope you like to go fast."

Payton's eyes shot from the bike to the helmet and back to him. "I've never been on one before. I don't know how."

"Really?"

"I always wanted to." She smiled, her eyes seeming to focus on some distant point from the past. "You used to ride that big bike around. I thought it looked so cool. Like such fun."

He remembered. It had been his cousin's. On loan for the summer while Nate worked a job the next county over. He'd seen her walking in town one sunny day and offered a ride. She'd wanted it, her expression reflecting pure desire, but she'd turned him down anyway. Looked guiltily behind her, as if she'd been afraid someone might have seen.

Someone with a heart condition she didn't want to worry.

He hadn't realized at the time. But that was what it had been. He couldn't help but wonder how many desires, big and small, she'd pushed aside to keep from upsetting her father. Or how devastating the loss of him must have been after sacrificing for so long—even if she'd known that, ultimately, the loss was inevitable.

Payton would have her fun now.

His blood pumped faster as he gave into the urge to play. Catching her wrist, he pulled her close. "So I'll be your *first.*"

A coy look from beneath the fringe of her lashes. "You will. Be gentle?"

Damn, he had fun with this woman.

"Don't worry. I'll start slow," he promised with a nip at her bottom lip before pulling the helmet over her head. "And if you get scared, just hold on tighter."

The pink tip of her tongue smoothed over his love bite, leaving a moist trail he wanted to follow with a lick of his own, but days like this one didn't last forever. So settling for a too-brief kiss instead, he winked and patted the seat behind him. "Let's hit it."

As it turned out, taking it slow wasn't an issue. Not in the slightest.

He'd expected Payton to be scared. To be holding on for dear life. Exhilarated by the experience, perhaps, but still maintaining some semblance of reserve. A healthy respect for her safety.

He had *not* expected the little minx in the leather jacket and flowing hippy skirt tucked around her thighs to be shamelessly feeling him up with one hand flat against his abdomen, the other snaking over the rise of his thigh. To nearly drive him over the edge with the breathy sounds of her pure, unadulterated delight as she begged him not to stop...to go faster...*yes, yes, yes, like that...*

Damn, how did she keep surprising him like this?

Taking everything he gave her and turning it into something beyond what he'd expected it to be.

He'd been after a quick spin down by the lake—the wind in his face with Payton's legs hugging his hips. That had been three hours ago.

One night. That had been over three weeks ago—

—and with no end in sight.

His back tensed beneath the press of her breasts.

Things were going too far. And he was *letting* it happen.

Even when he held back, she didn't… And the way Payton had fun—her enjoyment amplifying his own—made the willing surrender of his control an all too easy temptation to give into. But falling over the line in the sand he'd drawn—again and again, just because it felt good—was going to land him in a place where he didn't want to be. A place he'd have to walk away from. And that wasn't how he wanted it to go.

Daring fingers flexed and splayed over his thigh, moved ever closer to the hard ridge they'd provoked, forcing a strangled groan from Nate's throat as he throttled down the road toward his place.

Time for a reminder about who was in the driver's seat.

Time to take back control and set some limits. And if boundaries were going to be tested, it would happen the way he liked—on his terms. It was time to push *Payton* to extremes—make her pay for that wandering hand and finally get *her* to say "when".

CHAPTER FIFTEEN

MINUTES later they were rounding the top level of the parking garage in Nate's building. The sun burned low in the sky, casting the stark concrete supports in gilded rays.

"That was incredible!"

He barely heard her over the roar of the engine echoing through the structure and waited until he'd pulled to a stop and cut the engine to respond. Pushing the machine up on its stand, he grinned. "Yeah? Glad you had fun."

"I'm not sure fun even begins to describe it."

He stripped off his helmet and then turned to help her with hers. Damn, that smile was enough to drive a man to distraction.

And about that…he had some payback to attend to.

"Come here." He slipped one hand under her thigh and, the other around her back and, ignoring her squeak of surprise, pulled her around to straddle his lap. The gauzy fabric of her skirt bunched between them. Her heeled leather boots—looking decidedly bad-girl when paired with his bike—tucked behind her as she settled warm and soft against the hard-on he'd been battling for hours.

She stroked his jaw, brushing over the day's growth of stubble with a silky smile that had him responding even as he willed himself to heel. He shook his head, his gaze searching her face, trailing down her neck and body, and then returning to her eyes as he nuzzled into her palm, kissed the hollow and then ramped past "sweet" bringing a scrape of teeth into the action. He wanted her to know where this was going.

Payton's heart skittered to a halt as instant heat surged through her, twisting into a needy ache that left no part of her unaffected. Her breasts, her belly, her fingers and toes. Every fine hair that covered her body took notice, bowed beneath the desire born of his touch.

His tongue licked out as his blue eyes pierced her with his intent. Her breath sucked in. Her body coiled tight. And then he licked again, trailing a cool, wet path of erotic sensation in a circle around the first.

"We should go inside," she murmured, more than ready to let Nate take the exhilaration of the ride to the next level. This was a man who made her want everything. A man who, when merged with her, made her feel invincible. Unstoppable and completely alive.

One large hand snaked around her waist, while the other went to her nape, guiding her closer until their lips met in a soft brush, a teasing introduction after too long apart. Her fingers curled against his thighs, and he angled his head, taking the kiss deeper.

Willing and eager, she opened to him. Moaned against the claiming thrust of his tongue as he filled her mouth. So good but she wanted more than a taste. She wanted him everywhere and all at once. Everything he had. Everything he was.

Something was happening within her, something she knew better than to give into but couldn't seem to stop.

Take me. Make me yours.

The forbidden wish rose unbidden from the dark shadows of her mind.

Hold me. Forever.

When Nate let go of all his careful restraint, he gave her what she'd never had before. Showed her what she didn't know existed. It was incredible. Addictive. It was more than the physical. More than the mind-blowing sensation spearing through her at his slightest touch and deepest penetration.

But it wasn't what they'd agreed to. It wouldn't last. Only when he held her in his arms and stopped holding back, she felt as if, maybe, just maybe…it could.

Soft and wild. That was Payton. It was the sound of the cry that escaped when he caught her lip between his teeth, held and tugged the slightest bit. The sultry moan when he gripped her bottom, dragged her closer and drove his tongue deep into her mouth. Rocked harder as the muscles of her lean thighs bracketed him, flexing and tensing to the rhythm he'd set—until their breath came in fevered bursts between them. Desperate draws cut short by their need for more contact—deeper contact.

"Please…please…oh, God."

That's right. Just like that.

His hands fisted at her hips, seizing the delicate waistband of the panties that kept him from where he wanted to be. Sweet perfection tangled with his tongue, curling around, licking over him, sucking every bit of restraint from a mind that hadn't had much to begin with.

Control. That was what he was after. But her kiss stroked like a match-head over rough stone, igniting Nate in a flash flame. And there was no controlling the combustible desire when she opened to him, invited him in.

Tearing back from the kiss, he sucked air, tried to get a hold of himself. But all he could see were those soft wild curls swaying from side to side as Payton's mouth devoured his neck, his ears, his jaw, and then more when her fingers got in on the game—working the buttons of his shirt, with her lips following down his chest. Each heated kiss punctuated by her breathy pleas and silky declarations, "Nate, oh, Nate. What you do to me…want you…need you…don't stop…"

He couldn't stop. Didn't want to stop.

Don't ever stop.

His eyes opened. Had she said that? Or was it simply where his mind had taken him following his train of thought?

And then, somehow, she'd opened enough of the buttons to get the bulk of his chest free, and the little demon was licking at his nipple again. Her teeth grazing around it and then sucking with enough force the sensation pulled straight from his groin—where her deft fingers tugged at his straining fly and he was once again left panting through gritted teeth as he raced to keep up with her.

He was supposed to be holding the reins! It was Payton's turn to say "when".

"No." Hands clamped on her shoulders, he set her back against the fuel tank.

Her brows pulled together in pained confusion. "Why?"

"No condom." It was true, though only occurred to him as he'd grasped for an excuse to modify their positioning.

"I need to get on the pill," she groaned. Her heartrending cry of distress over their predicament would have been comical if his groin hadn't tightened to the point of pain at the forbidden memory of skin on silky smooth, wet skin. If he weren't totally caught up in her parted, kiss-swollen lips and the warm pants escaping them at a rate that damn near matched his speeding pulse.

"Upstairs," she urged, trying to sit up from her reclined position at the head of his bike.

Nate stopped her by running his hands up her splayed legs, still wrapped around him, and issuing a gruff, "Not yet."

He had a point to make and then, once she got it, he'd take her to the privacy of his apartment and spend the next twelve hours making her scream. But first, he took her hands and then brought them up to the handlebars at either side of her head. "Hold on."

Her eyes went wide and he waited for it, tasting the satisfaction of a success sure to come. This was where she told him "no". Where common sense and self-preservation prevailed and she realized she needed to slow down. Be more careful. Only her knees didn't pull closed, she didn't put a hand out to stop him.

She did as he'd commanded. She held on.

A part of him let out a cheer at the opportunity to take this fantasy come to life a step further. She'd break soon enough, but for now…

Backing down the seat to make his intent perfectly clear, he fingered a bit of her skirt and then flipped it back to expose her panties.

Turquoise. Lace.

Damp.

"Nate," she gasped.

Oh, yeah. Here it comes. "We should stop." Only then, nothing but the anxious shifting of her thighs, the soft musk of her arousal driving him past sanity.

Fine. Desperate times called for desperate measures. "Don't worry," he growled. "There isn't much traffic up here. I doubt anyone will catch us."

No way he could meet her eyes after that one—no one came up to his private garage level, ever—but he was all about pressing the advantage, so, eyes on those racy panties that should have come with a warning, he slid his arms beneath her legs.

This would do it.

He draped first one supple leg and then the other over his shoulders until he had her so erotically laid out he didn't know if he could last. But it wouldn't take much more. It couldn't.

He was taking back control. Showing her who was in charge— Except then he felt it, the slight dig of those killer-heeled boots at his back. Pulling him in.

Payton, Payton.

His hands tightened around her thighs and, slipping the damp scrap of her panties aside, he sank into her sweetness, tasted her cry and the pulse of her body's ready desire. It was insane and irrational, and yet—those stunned breathy gasps of pleasure, the widening of those deep brown eyes he couldn't stop watching—suddenly, he didn't want her to do anything but go with it.

She was desire mixed with an eager curiosity and sense of adventure that left him panting, straining, and demanded he step up to the challenge and make every damn minute they had before this ended the most exciting she'd ever experienced. He wanted her to let him take her as far as he possibly could.

He licked and kissed, circling outward until he felt her writhe beneath him and then working back in until he earned it again. Plumbing with deep thrusts of his tongue and nibbling with the softest graze of his teeth. He closed his mouth over that little bead and drew against her, tasting her cry on his tongue, increasing the strength of his pull with her escalating pleasure until her voice broke, her body quaked and spasmed and she came apart for him with the gift of her total abandon.

When she'd finished, he gathered her close. Ignoring the strain of his erection, he wound his fingers in the back of her hair. The hair that completely betrayed the wild woman inside. Hair that defied conformity, rebelling against every method of restraint imposed upon it. Escaping every bind. Sexy, beautiful, vibrant hair.

He unclasped the barrette she'd secured it with at the nape of her neck, releasing all that wild, soft rebellion into his hands. Sifting through the curls with his fingers as his tongue delved into the wet haven of her mouth.

So he couldn't control everything.

So what. Maybe he didn't want to. Maybe giving into

Payton for a while was just what he needed. Holding back only made him want her more, and at the rate they were going, it would be years before he got her out of his system enough to give her up.

CHAPTER SIXTEEN

NATE pulled a suit from his closet and laid it over the end of the bed where Payton lazed beneath the blankets. "I'll be back Wednesday evening. We can have a late dinner."

A pair of shorts, track pants, tee shirts and socks were stacked haphazardly within his case. Straightening the lot, he caught the languid stretch of a pale arm by the headboard, the shifting of a slender leg. Considered shoving the whole packing mess to the floor and using the bed for the purpose it was intended.

"How is it I've gotten spoiled on you in only one month?" came the quiet purr from amid the sheets. "Five days is so long."

Nate chuckled, taking her pout for the stroke to his ego it was. She'd miss him. They'd fallen into a habit of seeing each other every other day or so and this would be the longest they'd gone apart since their first night together. In all honesty, the break was probably overdue.

As good as being with Payton felt, something about all that rightness—the ease with which she fit into too many areas of his life—was making his skin itch. Making him tug at his tie and rebel against a confine without physical properties. He needed some space. As she'd said, it had been over a month.

His motions slowed and he stood, frozen, holding a boxed shirt suspended above his case.

More than twenty-eight days.

He shot a glance at Payton, searching for an answer to a question he didn't like.

He'd have known if she started her period.

No. No. He was being paranoid. She wasn't pregnant. Couldn't be. How many times had he heard some television or radio commercial touting on about each woman's body being different. They just hadn't been together long enough for him to know what kind of different to expect from hers.

Only suddenly he wanted to pilfer through her diary in search of those little circled numbers. Figure out exactly where she kept that critical information and make a note of it. Reassure himself he hadn't somehow made the most monumental mistake of his life and then play a quiet game of keep away during those most fertile times of the month.

There was no way. A matter of days would confirm it. Only he'd be gone for the next five.

"Nate?" Payton pushed to her elbows and the sheet slipped low across the swell of her breast.

He shoved his hands into his pockets, balled his fists and tried for casual. "Why don't you come with me?"

He'd wanted the space, and at that moment was nearly gasping for breathing room, but the idea of not knowing, not being sure—it was intolerable. He'd set up another trip in a week or two.

She sat straighter. "What?"

"I'm going to be busy with work. Meetings. Drinks and dinners. But eventually I'll have to sleep. And if I have a woman back in my room, they won't try taking me out to some seedy strip club this time. Besides, the shopping is supposed to be top-notch."

Silence rang through the room, bouncing around the slate walls, allowing his agitation to grow.

"Um, that's nice, and I wish I could," she offered at last, "but I take vacations over school breaks."

His jaw set, his focus narrowed. "Call in sick."

She began smoothing one corner of the sheet between her fingers. "I've got plans with my family."

"You could see them anytime."

Her gaze slid away, the turn of her head shutting him out. She looked uncomfortable. As if whatever she was thinking wasn't something she wanted to share. And he was hanging every hope on it being some neurotic hang-up about discussing her menstrual cycle.

"I—well—"

This was ridiculous. He was railroading her into a trip he didn't want her to come on rather than just asking. Man up. "Your period?"

"What?"

"Are you expecting it? Is that why you don't want to come?"

Shifting to sit akimbo, Payton cocked her head in a way where Nate could almost see her calculating dates. Whatever excuse she'd been ready to offer, that wasn't it. Just as well she had a reason to stay behind, particularly since he'd broached the subject and had her on the right track now.

"Actually, yes. In the next few days." Then she squinted an eye at him. "Awfully intuitive. Do you have any hang-ups at all?"

He laughed as if she'd made some great joke, covering the relief that washed through him with tsunami force. "Not about that kind of thing. It's a period. Big deal. Women get them."

It was when they didn't get them, you had something to worry about.

She wrinkled her nose. "But you grew up in a house with just your father. No sisters. And yet, you're miles beyond what Brandt or Clint could handle."

Nate shrugged, feeling lighter than he had in days. "It's probably as much to do with my dad as anything else. Being the educator, he wasn't really one to shy away from a topic because it happened to apply more specifically to the other gender. And because my mom wasn't around to give the female perspective, he invariably felt an obligation to be as forthright as possible. The man was a chronic over-compensator."

Payton laughed and held out her hand. "Tee shirt?"

Nate pulled one from his bag and handed it over.

"You know, you've never really told me about your mom. She was gone by the time we met. But beyond that..."

And here he thought things were turning around. "What do you want to know?"

She had a right to ask. It wasn't any big deal, just not his favorite topic.

"What happened to her?"

"She took off when I was five. Life with Dad and me wasn't right for her. She wanted something different, I guess. Hell, I don't know, something else."

A little line crinkled between her brows, suggesting she didn't like where the story was going. But she needn't have worried, there wasn't much more than what he'd already said.

Leaning across the bed, he dropped a kiss on her knee. "It wasn't too bad. She'd checked out long before she actually left, so it wasn't like we'd suddenly lost something we didn't know how to live without."

"But what did she do? Where did she go?" He could all but see the unspoken question painted across her face. *"How could she leave you?"*

"I don't know where she ended up. Dad did, for a while at least—he made sure she was okay. You know how he is. But for me, once she left, that was it."

"But she's your mother. She knew you. Loved you."

A vision of a pretty smile and distracted eyes slipped through his memory. Soft hair and a nice smell. Remote. Unavailable. Watching her stare out the window, the door... down the road.

Nate zipped the bag and hefted it to the floor before meeting Payton's waiting eyes. She hurt for him. He could see it there, but she didn't need to. "Payton, some people aren't cut out to have a family. I don't think my mom was a bad person, I think she just didn't understand the way she was until it was too late." Deficient. Same as him.

Payton couldn't imagine it. Giving a child five years of attachment and then ripping it away. What did that do to a little boy? What did it do to the man he became? "Is that why you don't—?"

"Does it really matter?"

Maybe it did. Her lips parted to press the question, but the quick shake of Nate's head and hardening of his eyes told her not to.

Ignoring the pinch in her heart, she pushed a smile to lips rebelling against it and tried for the make-light conversation that always smoothed over those sticky moments. "So you've got everything you need for the trip? Razor, toothbrush, stack of singles for the strip club?"

Nate barked out a laugh, his head hang-dog low. "What kind of man do you think I am?" Then, turning that impish blue glint of mischief on her, he grabbed her ankle and pulled her to him. "It's a stack of fives, baby."

"So bad," she murmured, pulling him down to her mouth for a kiss. And like that they were fine. Casual and easy. "And, I know, I like it." She loved it. As she knew she loved him, even though she wasn't supposed to.

Two nights later, Payton curled into the corner of the sofa, phone held to her ear as Nate recounted his botched attempt to evade the strip club the evening before. Eyes closed, she listened to his voice, missing the feel of his arms around her. "I told you what would happen if you didn't come with me."

She sighed. "Poor Nate. The things you suffer for the love of your business."

"She mocks."

"She does. But only a little." She smiled at Nate's low chuckle. "I miss you."

"You, too. When's dinner with your mom and Brandt?"

"Tomorrow night. I'll drive out after school." She pulled the throw higher and tucked her legs beneath her. "It's still strange going home, knowing my father won't be there. You'd think after a year I'd be used to it."

"I think it's perfectly normal. You grew up in that house with him. In your heart, he's a part of it. I'm sorry it hurts, though."

She nodded, simply wishing Nate could be there with her before she thought better of it. Brandt would love that, particularly since this would be the first time she actually had to face him since her relationship began. She took a deep breath, knowing it was time for the call to come to an end. She was getting wistful and both of them needed to get up early the next morning. "Well," she sighed, stretching across the cushions where she'd gone lax under the spell of his voice. "I better let you go."

"Hey, Payton, one more thing?"

"Mmm-hmm?" God, she missed him.

"What we were talking about the other morning," he began, the soothing tone of his voice taking on an efficient business-like edge. "Your period—did you get it?"

She blinked, mildly surprised by his question. "Um, yes, I did. Today actually."

"Good." A long breath filtered through the line, and she pulled the phone from her ear, staring at the receiver. A moment of insecurity touched her with the nagging sensation that last question had been the purpose of the whole call. But then she thought of the circumstances that had brought them together. A pregnancy. A child. Six months of the cruelest uncertainty.

She couldn't blame him for being concerned and suddenly felt immensely grateful this wasn't one of those months she simply missed her period altogether.

"Don't worry, Nate. Everything's fine."

"Have some ice cream or binge on something disgusting or whatever you women do. I'll see you in a few days."

CHAPTER SEVENTEEN

"Mom, Brandt's pulling up," Payton called, watching from the front window as the black Escalade pulled into the circular drive. It had been weeks since she'd seen Brandt and, aside from the one brusque call she'd received about the folly of getting involved with a man like Nate, he'd been unusually quiet as of late, burying himself deep in the running of Liss Industries. Doing well. Her father would have been proud.

Heading to the foyer, she heard the thud of a car door and then stalled mid-step at the sound of another.

A moment later the front door swung open wide and her brother strode in, a cavalier grin on his face and Clint on his heels.

Payton's back straightened, her jaw setting hard.

"Hey, Payton," Brandt offered with a jut of his chin by way of greeting as he crossed to take her in quick hug. "Hope you don't mind, I've brought Clint along for dinner."

She raised a cool brow at her brother as betrayal shot hot through her veins. "I see." She did mind. Very much, in fact, but when had anything as trivial as her opinion ever stopped her brother before?

Clint crossed to her and dropped a chaste kiss to her cheek. "Don't blame Brandt. I asked him to arrange this. Things didn't go the way I'd intended the last time we spoke—" He broke off, letting out a strained breath before turning back to her. "And my behavior was unacceptable. But I'm asking you for a chance to talk. Privately."

She looked from Clint to Brandt and then to her mother, who was descending the wide staircase. "I'm here to have dinner with my family."

"Nonsense," her mother interjected, urging her to understand with her eyes. "There's time enough for everyone. Brandt's taking me over to the store to pick up something to go with the lamb. It'll give you two a chance to talk and then we'll have dinner after we get back."

Brandt crossed his arms over his chest. "Don't be difficult about this, Payton. I think it's the least you can do considering the way these last weeks have played out. In fact, I'd say you owe it to Clint here."

Payton swallowed, looking past her overbearing brother to the door she wished she'd never ventured through this evening. Releasing a short breath, she nodded, taking a step back from Clint even as she agreed to speak with him. She didn't want any misread signals. Any misunderstandings. But she did feel bad about the way she'd handled the Nate situation with him.

Clint acknowledged with a pained twist of his lips and a resigned nod. Extending one arm toward the living room, he gave her the space to pass. Then turned to Brandt and her mother. "I appreciate this."

Payton crossed the ancient oriental and perched at the edge of a wingback chair, ankles crossed, hands folded neatly in her lap. Clint followed her into the room and, catching sight of her there, paused, a small smile touching his lips. "You look beautiful."

"Thank you, but—"

He held up a hand and walked over to the chair opposite her. "Merely stating the facts." Then after a pause, "How did we get here, Payton? So far from where we're supposed to be."

He looked up at her. "I've given you time, but this business with Nate Evans has gone too far."

Payton shook her head. "What's happening with Nate is none of your business—"

"Fine." He leaned forward. "Forget him. He's not important anyway. Not for our future. All I care about is us. You and me. Going forward. I know after your father passed away you had a tough time. You needed…space…to adjust. And I gave it to you."

They'd broken up. She'd told him it was over. Not that she needed space. But Clint wouldn't see it that way. He'd chalked her behavior up to a reaction to her father's death. And maybe it had been, but that didn't change the fact that she'd made the right choice in leaving him.

"I don't love you, Clint."

He shook his head, not willing to hear. Or maybe not caring. "We were good together. Right."

She felt the familiar stab of frustration, bit back the hot denial that rushed to her lips, knowing it would be dismissed as irrational. Pulling her composure around her, she met his stare. "No. We were never that good or that right together. Only you couldn't see it and I didn't want to admit it. But I knew. Even before Daddy… A part of me wouldn't let us go forward, wouldn't talk about marriage when you brought it up… I wanted to be happy about what we had. I wanted to see what everyone else saw. How perfect we were together. But I wasn't being honest with myself or you. I'm so sorry, Clint."

"You realize what you're giving up here?"

She nodded. A life where she felt trapped by a man who, though decent enough, didn't really care to know her.

"I do."

* * *

Knock, knock knock, knock… "Payton, open up."

Brandt. He must have hopped in his car the minute he got back to the house and discovered she'd left.

The last thing she wanted was to continue this little intervention here at home. She'd do about anything to dodge her big brother coming down on her with all his disappointment and bullying. Maybe if she didn't answer he'd just go.

"Don't bother hiding. I know you're in there." Of course he did. Her car was parked outside and she was the sole occupant of the third floor, with every light in the apartment shining down on the street below.

Returning the paperback she'd just picked up to the To Be Read pile beside her couch, she pushed to her feet and walked to the door in time to hear the lock tumble as Brandt made use of the keys she sorely regretted giving him.

"Unless you've got a bolt cutter in there, just give me a second." She slipped the chain and stepped back, arms crossed, ready to face him down. "You can't let yourself in here any time you want."

Brandt swung the door open and met her determined stare, raising it with a measure of disappointment only their mother could rival. "You've done it now. Clint's through."

"I wasn't trying to hurt him, Brandt. But I'm glad he finally believes me."

"You're throwing away your future for some…fling. You know that's what it is, right? Mr. Bachelor of the year…bad-boy billionaire Nate Evans. Are you stupid? You know how he gets those names, right? By pricking around."

"Shut up, Brandt. You don't know what's between Nate and I—"

"Yeah, and I don't want to know, except that, with Dad gone, I'm the one looking out for you."

She let out a harsh breath. "I don't need anyone looking out for me. Especially someone who can't understand the choices I'm making in my life."

She mumbled under her breath, walking away.

"Did you just call me a 'stupid jerk'?"

She had. Heat splashed her cheeks, but, unwilling to back down, she spun on him. "If the shoe fits…"

Only then the absurdity of her muttered insult hit them both. The tension and starch seemed to slip from her brother's shoulders and he leaned back into the wall behind him. Pressing the heels of his palms into his brows, he let out a heavy breath. "I know how you feel, Payton. About Dad. About trying to be perfect for so long. It wears on you and all that pressure makes you resentful. Only you know you can't get angry at him. The weak heart wasn't something he could help. So you keep trying to do the right thing. Take care of him. Be good. Try harder… Except, after all that effort, he goes and dies anyway. It was a raw deal. I know that."

Tears bit at the backs of her eyes as her bully-big-brother voiced what her heart had been sobbing for a year. "It's like everything I did, all the right choices I made were for nothing."

"So now you want to be bad for a while? Is that what this is with Nate? With the apartment? Clint? Every major decision you've made in the last year has been the sort of thing Dad would have hated. Are you trying to get even with him? Show him what happens when he doesn't hold up his end of the bargain and live?"

Her throat was so dry, she didn't think she could speak. She shook her head, blinking away the welling tears. "No. It's about being true to myself. Living my own life. Mine. Not his. The job I want. The apartment I can afford." *The man I love.*

Brandt scanned her apartment, as though doubting her word. Then pushed off the wall and stuffed his hands deep into his pockets. "You know, on the way over to Mom's, Clint and I were talking about when you two started dating. Apparently he'd asked you what you wanted out of a relationship."

Her breath pulled in with a slow ache. She knew where this was going.

"You said, 'Family and security, trust and partnership.' I think he figured out he wanted to marry you that night."

She'd known it, too. Looked at Clint and thought he was exactly the right sort of man to make a life with. And yet every time he'd brought up marriage, she'd shied away.

As if following her thoughts, Brandt offered, "Even if Clint wasn't the one. You gave him an honest answer, didn't you? You still want those things?"

When she didn't answer, Brandt's scowl deepened and the understanding man who might have been her friend a moment ago transformed back into the brother frustrated with the mess his little sister was making of her life. "What does Nate Evans think about those wants? I'm assuming he knows. Or did this 'honest life' you're so keen on living not include being honest with him?"

"It's not like that with Nate. Neither one of us is interested in marriage or forever right now."

Brandt let out a short laugh. "Right. Who are you lying to now, Payton?"

Her mouth burst open in denial, but already he'd gone on. "Have you been honest with that guy for one minute since you started whatever the hell it is you're doing together? Does he have any idea how long you've been pining for him? I'd be willing to bet a sizable chunk of Liss shares that he doesn't. Just like I'd bet he doesn't know how showing up in the papers has affected your work environment—the flak you take for it."

"Things have been better at work lately—"

"I'm glad to hear it, but *come on*, *Payton*, the last time we talked about this you were hell-bent on getting out of the media spotlight. Swearing up and down that wedding you and Evans were caught at would be the last high-profile event. You were desperate. And yet, I think I've seen your name or face in the news more times over the last month than I have in the last year."

"It's different now."

"Why?" he challenged. "Because you're in love?"

"Things are good with Nate. We both knew what we were getting into with this relationship and we're both fine with it."

He took a deep breath and shoved off the wall. Stopping at the door, he turned to her. "Payton, if you have to lie to me, that's one thing. You want to lie to Nate Evans?" He touched the single bump at the bridge of his nose. "Be my guest. Just do me a favor and don't lie to yourself."

The door swung closed with a thud. The lock tumbled and then even the muffled fall of his steps left her. Alone, she faced the uneasy revelation that perhaps Brandt had seen her more clearly than she'd ever given him credit for.

CHAPTER EIGHTEEN

SOMETHING was wrong with Payton.

Nate stood by the exit watching the dinner crowd. The up-scale Mexican restaurant was one of his favorites and Payton had mentioned it as one of hers as well, but tonight she'd barely had a bite of her food and her glass of wine sat all but untouched on the table.

He'd gone to her place straight from O'Hare, ready to pick up where they'd left off almost a week before. The trip had been a success and he was in the mood for a celebration. But even before they'd made it to the car he'd sensed something *off*. They'd talked easily enough, laughed and caught up, but every few minutes her attention would drift, leaving him to wonder where she'd gone.

By the time he closed out the bill his frustration had met its limit and he was ready for answers.

Hitting the sidewalk, Payton looked back at him apologetically. "I'm sorry. I just—" Breaking off with a shake of her head, she stared down the street.

A quiet alarm began to sound in the back of his mind. Obviously something happened while he'd been gone, and whatever it was had her anxious and refusing to meet his eyes. He didn't want to think it, but if he didn't know her better he'd say her behavior smacked of guilt. "What's going on?"

Hugging her arms around her waist, she shivered. "Can we walk a minute?"

He tucked her under his arm, guiding her around the Friday-night pedestrian traffic. As he slowed his stride to match hers his mind ran through the little he knew. She'd been fine when he spoke to her the other night. Laughing and easy. No halting exchanges or strained silence. But that had been three days ago and he hadn't spoken to her since. He should have called again, checked in, but he'd gotten busy, caught up in the workings of a new deal— And he'd wanted the space. The distance.

But just for the few days. Now that he was back he wanted Payton laughing and sexy and giving him everything that threatened to be too much. And she wasn't.

Halfway down the block she turned to him. "I'm being stupid. It's nerves is all—I don't want—" She took a deep breath and shook her head. "The other night I was supposed to have dinner with my family, only we didn't actually make it that far. Brandt decided to bring Clint with him—"

Clint. Tension wrapped tight around his chest, making it difficult to breathe. The guy who'd wanted to marry her. The guy who'd grabbed her in the middle of a charity reception.

"So you left?" he prompted, knowing she hadn't.

"No. My mother and Brandt left, so Clint and I could talk."

"They left you alone with him." Heat crawled up his throat and face as he let loose a violent curse. Immediately he was pushing up her sleeves, trying to see the skin on her arms through the wash of red nearly blinding him. "If he hurt you—" If that was the reason, what she was afraid to tell him—

"No, he didn't touch me. Nate, please." She caught his hand in hers. "I'm fine."

"You are not fine," he growled, barely managing to contain

himself from bellowing. "You're worrying over something, refusing to look me in the eye. And I can't tell if it's because you've done something you think is going to hurt me or because someone else has done something and you think I'm going to hurt them. So *tell me what happened*."

Her chin jerked back in surprise, but quickly she answered. "I was upset, but Clint obviously needed some closure, which I believe he finally got. And when we were through talking, I didn't want to wait around for Mom and Brandt to start in on me again. So I left. Only Brandt followed me home."

"What the hell is that guy's problem?" he roared in frustration, glaring at the sky.

Silence answered, drew out for a moment, and then, "He thinks I'm not being honest about what's going on between us. About what being with you means to me." She took a steadying breath before meeting his eyes again. "And…maybe he's right."

With that the red haze receded, leaving him with an understanding of what was behind Payton's distress. No one had hurt her. At least not yet.

"Because you want…more." Marriage. A family. More than a good time for as long as it held up.

"I do."

He should have seen it coming. Hell, he'd known from the start what her priorities were, that long term they didn't mesh with his. Damn it, he didn't want this now. He just wanted Payton back in his arms after days apart. He wanted her laughing and giving him her smart mouth and her soft body. He wanted the good time. The easy ride.

But the easy ride was over.

She was quiet beside him, her head pressed into her palms. Smoothing a hand down her curls, he pulled her into his chest. "There's nothing wrong with wanting those things, Payton." He looked up at the black night, took a breath of the bracing air and forced himself to say the rest. "So long as you aren't waiting to find them with me."

It was only the barest of movements. No more than the slightest stiffening of her body. But he felt it. He closed his eyes, knowing what he had to say next.

Clearing his throat, he took a step back.

Those brown eyes stared up at him, waiting. Wounded. She knew what was coming. Knew they'd agreed to stop before things got serious. Stupid. As if it hadn't been serious with Payton from the start.

Her lips parted and she whispered a single word. "Don't."

He didn't want to do this.

"Do you think maybe it's time to stop?" he asked, taking her hand in his. She was shaking her head no, but it hadn't really been a question. He caught her cheek in his hand, slid his fingers into that wild hair. "I don't want to hurt you."

Too late.

"Then don't." Her hands covered his chest as though it would be enough to keep him there. Hell. She didn't understand that the organ beneath her hands didn't work the way she needed it to.

"Payton—"

"Aren't you having fun?" Her big brown eyes turned to liquid pools, that kissable bottom lip of hers beginning to tremble. "Hasn't it been good?"

"You know I am. That it has." Damn it, he didn't want to see her cry—didn't want to be the reason for her tears.

"Because, I'm having fun with you. Like I've never had before." Her words coupled with the glitter of wet tears on her lashes would have been laughable, except for the pain behind them. Cutting through him, she wiped at her eye with the back of a wrist. "All I need is the chance that maybe—"

"I care about you. More than I've cared about anyone else."

Only that didn't change the fact that love didn't happen for him. He'd told her about his mother, but what he should have spelled out was he was just like her. His inability to connect completely in the romantic arena was more than a habit born from defense or disgust at being the center of media speculation. More than a convenience too comfortable to investigate, though, in all honesty, it had been that, too. Why bother trying to overcome something that worked just fine for him? He hadn't cared until now.

"Isn't that something? Isn't it enough to wait and see? Yes, I want marriage…someday. But I've been so careful about everything for so long, I'm willing to take a risk for you. I would wait."

He knew she would. If he gave her any hope at all, she'd spend years waiting for something that, in all likelihood, he would never be able to give her. She might be willing to take that risk, but he wasn't. Not with her heart. Her life. Her happiness.

She wanted the white picket fence and the pram around the park. And he wanted her to have it. Even if it meant letting her go so someone else could give it to her.

"I'm sorry, sweetheart." And that was when the first camera flashed and the shutters began snapping.

CHAPTER NINETEEN

PAYTON'S gown crinkled, gaping in falls of stiff, creased blue paper as she sat atop the padded exam table, legs crossed with as much lady-like decorum as she could muster given the circumstances. She was crabby. Sick and depressed. Fighting what had become a perpetual state of lethargy for weeks. But she wouldn't give in to it—surrender to the call of her bed simply because she'd been dumped.

It happened. To everyone, she was told.

Though usually not with the media there to witness the critical moment. But what did she really care if they'd splashed the portrait of her heartbreak across the newsstands? Or if Nate was pictured almost daily looking every bit the modern-day rake the papers made him out to be. The only thing that mattered was the affair was over and her life had to go on.

So she kept busy. Waited for the heartrending pain to pass. For her lip to finally stiffen up. For that promised time when another fish from the sea of men might actually appeal to her. She had a job she was passionate about and new friends who wouldn't let her breakup come between them. And even her fellow teachers had reached out to her in spite of the reporters trolling the block. So she got up every day and went to work and kept her appointments.

Like this one she'd scheduled weeks ago.

Dr. Thoms breezed into the room, pumped a handful of

sanitizer into her palm and rubbed it in as she scanned the electronic chart on her worktable. "So this is a regular check up today, and I see you'd called about beginning an oral contraceptive."

Payton's knuckles whitened as she gripped the table's edge, tears threatening again. Please, God, not in the gynecologist's office. They'd be writing her a referral to another kind of doctor altogether if she started sobbing here. "Um, yes, but..."

"Were you thinking primarily about birth control or to regulate your periods?"

Her ears pricked up. Of course she'd known the pill could do both, but she'd never really been inconvenienced enough to consider it. Only now, after weeks of bouncing all over the place emotionally, physically feeling the signs of an impending cycle then barely having one at all... This could be the answer to at least one of her problems. Albeit the most minor.

"Regulating my periods." Since she couldn't imagine ever having sex again. At least with anyone other than Nate...and she was doing her very best not to imagine that.

Thankfully, Dr. Thoms seemed oblivious to her inner turmoil and, focused on the task at hand, continued on. "Okay, then. So how are you feeling overall?"

Sad. Lonely. Stunned beyond belief that Nate could walk away from what they'd had so easily. Stunned even more by the physical toll their breakup was taking on her. "A little run-down, but it's not—no. I'm fine."

"Run-down? Any fever, runny nose, sore throat, upset stomach?"

"My stomach's been off, but I think it's more nerves than anything. And I'm beat." Then going for a little levity, she added, "Just sick and tired of being sick and tired."

Only it fell as flat as everything else.

Ignoring the weak joke, Dr. Thoms stared at her with that placid smile in place. "And when was your last period?"

"I had it for about a day, two and a half weeks ago."

Cool eyes met hers over the top of the chart. "Just a day? Was it heavy? Light?"

The temperature in the room dropped.

Payton didn't like the look she was getting. Her hand went to her stomach again, and those eyes narrowed ever so slightly, following the motion.

"Light." And then she hastily added, "But it's not that unusual. My cycle isn't exactly like clockwork. And we were using protection, so I really don't think you need to worry."

"Mmm-hmm." The doctor typed in a few notes. "Any dizzy spells, unusual tenderness in your breasts, mood swings, cravings or loss of appetite?"

The questions hit her like rapid-fire artillery. Each punching a bigger hole through her façade of calm.

Yes…yes…yes…

Oh, God, it couldn't be. "Doctor, I see where you're going with this, but I can't be—" She broke off, unwilling to even say the words. Desperately trying not to even think them.

Failing.

Pregnant.

Pregnant with a tiny, little piece of Nate growing inside her.

Her eyes pinched shut as she sucked air, willing the precious image away. She couldn't want it to be true, shouldn't be hoping it into existence. But something instinctual stirred to life within her, and on the deepest level she knew it was too late for hopes or wishes to make any difference at all.

"What am I going to do?"

Responding to a question far more encompassing than it had been interpreted, Dr. Thoms answered simply, "You're going to start by taking a pregnancy test."

* * *

Two hours later, the results had been confirmed and an ultrasound done to determine gestation. Payton walked the downtown streets in a daze, barely registering the blare of midday traffic, screeching tires and shouts for taxis as each step brought her closer to a conversation she'd never anticipated having. Explaining to Nate that his biggest fear—his worst nightmare and the horrific scenario he'd so recently escaped—had once again become a reality.

How would he react to the news?

She knew he'd be doing the math, same as she. Wondering if they'd ever had a chance or if their fate had been sealed from that very first night. He'd wonder if the fun and games had been worth it.

Know they hadn't.

The clap of thunder broke through her reverie, pulling her eyes to the gunmetal-gray sky and the steel and glass tower slicing into it. Nate's building.

Wrapping her arms around her waist, she tried to stave off the numbing cold seeping beneath her skin.

Would he hate her?

"Payton, is that you?"

She turned toward the lilting voice and found herself face to face with Nate's longtime assistant.

"Deborah, how are you?" she asked, embarrassed to be caught standing this way by the fifty-ish woman with a soft heart and mind too sharp to chalk her presence there up to coincidence.

"Are you headed up to see Nate?"

She opened her mouth, then simply shut it again. Was she? She'd come here to tell him about the baby, but now that she stood so close to her destination, she couldn't do it. Not like this. Nate deserved better than to have the news dropped in his lap between afternoon meetings. He'd always tried to do right by her, and she owed him, at least, a reasonable conversation in private. The news would devastate him—shatter the life he'd worked so hard to protect. The life he'd sacrificed her to preserve.

Finally, she forced enough air from her lungs to form words. "No. I thought I'd stop in, but I…" she held up her left arm, without looking to see she wasn't wearing a watch "…I don't have time after all."

Compassion shone in the older woman's eyes as she reached out and squeezed Payton's numb hand. "You're shivering, sweetheart." Then turning up her own collar against the wind and chill, she nodded toward the building behind her. "Wouldn't you like to come inside for a coffee?"

The seconds passed as Payton stared at the lobby doors, followed the lines of the architectural mammoth dominating the landscape around it. "No, thank you. I'm going home. Don't worry."

With a reluctant nod, Deborah turned down the sidewalk and went on her way.

Payton smoothed a hand over the still-flat plane of her belly and, eyes fixed on the building that so reflected its owner, the dizzying truth of what would happen when Nate found out she was pregnant hit her full in the face. If she didn't have a rock-solid plan for her future in place before she told him the news, Nate Evans would take over and make one for her.

CHAPTER TWENTY

THE piercing whistle of steam escaping the kettle was broken by the repetitive buzz of her security intercom. She turned off the gas and dashed down the hall. "Hello?"

"It's Nate. Let me up."

She stared blankly at the little white box mounted on her wall. Too soon. She was supposed to have hours more. He couldn't be here already.

Then brain function kicked in and she pushed the "entry" button and swung open the front door. Nate, taking the stairs two at a time, rounded her landing in a matter of seconds. He looked tired and impatient and more handsome than any man had a right to be as he strode to her door, taking in the length of her in a sweeping head-to-toe scan that nearly rocked her back with its intensity. For one precious heartbeat, she thought he'd come for them. That he'd realized he loved her, too. That he missed her enough he couldn't stay away—

"What's wrong?" he demanded, pushing into her apartment.

She stepped aside, closing her eyes before Nate could catch the disappointment there. Obviously, Deborah had spoken to him. She'd suspected it would happen and even turned the phone to voice mail in anticipation of a call, but she hadn't expected him to show up at her door in less than an hour's time. She wasn't prepared to face him yet, only Nate caught her arm, his hold gentle but firm as he forced her to meet his stare. "What's wrong?" he asked more urgently.

I'm pregnant.

It was the simple answer. And yet she couldn't make herself say the words. Not yet.

This much she'd decided.

"I'm sorry, I was going to call. You didn't need to rush over—"

Nate's brows drew down. His mouth pinching flat for a beat. "Deborah told me you'd been standing outside the building…crying. I cancelled my afternoon to come over here so don't give me the runaround."

Wincing at the cut of his sharp tone, she took a bracing breath. "I was thinking about us."

She half expected him to check his watch, see if he could make it back to the office to finish up one of those meetings after all. But he held steady, if not somewhat wary. "Us?"

Us. The two of them. The way it had been when they were together, creating the one who would make three. "I miss you."

Nate raked a hand through his hair, rubbed the back of his head with the rough strokes of a man trying to make sense of something exasperating beyond explanation. "I miss you, too, sweetheart. But we talked about this and decided if there was any chance for us to end up friends down the road…we need to give each other time apart now."

She knew all that. As the she knew the answer to her next question, too—the only question that mattered, the one that would decide everything—but had to ask it anyway. Had to hear him say the words aloud.

She swallowed and then, aching with a desperate heartfelt need, forced the words past her lips. "Do you love me?"

Her breath held, painful and hope-swollen within her chest

as she watched his eyes widen, felt the lingering caress of his gaze as it stroked over her cheeks, lips and eyes.

Please, she begged with every part of her heart, body and soul.

And when he didn't answer, she couldn't stop herself from saying more. Adding to her plea, her heartbreak and humiliation. "What we had was good." He couldn't have forgotten. "I miss it. I miss you." Maybe all he needed was to know. "And I thought after you've had some time away." She had to try. "Some space." Give him every chance. "That you might—"

"Payton, stop. Don't do this to yourself." It was blunt and cruel. But he couldn't stand the idea of prolonging her questions or suffering any longer. "Nothing's changed. And it won't."

Payton banded her arms over her slim waist and nodded. Stiff. "Okay," she whispered on a catch of breath that left him wrecked. She shook her head, the slight motion freeing a solitary tear to escape down the delicate slope of her cheek. "That's what I needed to know."

Damn it, this wasn't how he wanted it to go.

He wanted the fantasy they'd talked about those few months ago. The scenario where the passion between them died a natural death, going peacefully in its sleep some night, months and months from now. The deal where they woke to the friendship that had always been there.

Where, when he saw her crying, reaching out to touch her wouldn't just make it worse for both of them.

Her head fell forward into the cradle of her palm and she let out a shuddering breath he felt through his entire being. His fists clenched, once. Twice, before he physically couldn't stand to let her suffer there alone and reached for her—

"I'm pregnant."

His hand dropped to his side as the air left his lungs in a painful whoosh.

Time stood still and, paralyzed, helpless to stop it, he felt the foundation of his world begin to slide beneath his feet.

No.

This couldn't be happening. Not again. It was impossible—except the defeated set to Payton's shoulders told him it wasn't.

She turned her head in profile, not quite meeting his eyes, and whispered, "I'm so sorry."

Quietly she walked from the room, leaving him to absorb the truth of the situation. She was pregnant.

Alone, Nate walked to the window, stared at the rain beating down on the glass and wondered how after so little time he'd found himself brought full circle. And with the very woman he'd thought would help him leave the nightmare behind.

Ironic.

Fate's little way of giving him the finger, he supposed.

The suspicions that had plagued him from the first minutes following Annegret's teary pregnancy confession lurked in the shadows of his memory, daring him to revisit them. But to all those dark scenarios came the same resounding, "No." This wasn't some mercenary fortune hunter coming to him pregnant. It was Payton. So good even when she wanted to be bad, Payton. If she said there was a baby, there was. And without question it was his.

He shook his head, stunned. How could the entire world change in less than an hour? That was all it had been since Deborah called his direct line from her lunch break. She'd found Payton shaking in the cold outside his building, her red-rimmed eyes looking lost and scared. He'd raced to her apartment, unable to maintain the distance they'd discussed for fear something had happened.

But she'd looked fine when he arrived and he'd been angry

he'd had to see her. Had to see the hurt in her eyes when he didn't want to think about her hurting at all.

He'd wanted her to go away. Find someone else. Forget about him.

Only she hadn't been as fine as he'd thought, and now her going away was no longer an option. She'd never find the life she deserved and he was angry all over again.

How the hell could it have happened? The way he'd been going through condoms while they were together, he should have bought stock in the company. He'd been in charge of the protection and they'd used it every time—except that once.

His gut clenched, guilt working its way up his throat like bile.

He'd stopped before he'd come, found a condom and then returned to finish what he'd started. But unprotected penetration of any kind could result in pregnancy. And he'd been so damn careless. Even after everything he'd been through. Even knowing better.

He'd done this to them.

Eyes fixed on the gray-washed day beyond the glass, he pulled his phone from his pocket and brushed a thumb across the screen to bring up Deborah.

"I need you to get Arnie on the line for me. And then see what it takes to get married in Illinois."

CHAPTER TWENTY-ONE

PAYTON sat at the kitchen table, her gaze fixed on the cooling mug of tea between her palms. She'd left Nate in the living room nearly a half-hour before. After a time, she'd heard the baritone clip of his voice as he began making calls. Then a moment ago silence resumed.

The hardwood groaned its quiet protest under the weight of his approach and then Nate's dark form filled the doorway. Arms braced against the frame like a looming threat, he pressed into the room without entering.

"I found out this morning at my doctor's," she volunteered, figuring it as good a place to start as any.

Concern furrowed his brow. "Are you okay?"

It didn't surprise her; there'd never been a question of caring. Only of degree.

"Yes. It was time for my annual and I'd mentioned getting on the pill when I booked the appointment. One thing led to another and then…I knew." She picked up the mug and took a lukewarm sip, wishing for the soothing relief the picture on the box promised. "It happened within that first week or two."

Nate shouldered through the door and dropped into the seat across the table, meeting her eyes for the first time since she'd told him she was pregnant. The cold acceptance in his gaze should have hurt, but the pain was gone—replaced by a hollow kind of numb that had taken hold after she'd ripped her soul open, exposing the most tender, vulnerable part of herself to him. Begging him to love her. The blissful void of emotion wouldn't last, but she'd savor every moment while it did.

He reached across the table and wrapped his fingers around hers in a hold that felt stiff, uncomfortably dutiful. "Do you have a doctor? An OB for the pregnancy?"

She shook her head. Noted the lines deepening across his forehead and around his mouth.

His voice lowered, taking on a hard edge she could hear him fighting. "But you *are* getting one."

Then she understood what he was asking—if she planned to keep their child. "I've known about the baby for less than one day, Nate. The fact that I haven't gotten a doctor yet doesn't mean anything except that I need to do some research before selecting one."

His eyes cleared with relief. "I'm sorry, I just—" He shook his head and blew out a strained breath. "It's important. I have to ask certain things."

She nodded, her neck sore from the tension that had gripped her hours ago.

"I'm meeting with Arnie tomorrow about changing my will and drawing up a prenuptial agreement for us."

Payton fought an empty smile, noting his subtle pairing of death and marriage. Her mouth opened to set him straight, but he had his hand out, ready to cut her off.

"You know I'm going to be fair. The details are flexible, but I'm non-negotiable on the point of the agreement itself."

She couldn't care less about a prenuptial agreement. Because they wouldn't need one.

"I'm not marrying you." No satisfaction came from the words, only the bone-deep certainty that they were true.

"Don't be like this, Payton. It's important. An agreement will protect us both."

"Nate, it's not about the prenup. *I'm not marrying you.*"

His eyes narrowed on her. "What are you talking about? You're pregnant. Of course you are."

"No."

She saw the moment it clicked for him. When the pieces fell into place and a dark shadow fell across his hardening features. "The questions. You weren't worrying about me stepping up. It was a test. A trap. Making me tell you—" His eyes pinched shut, a vein popping to life along his temple. "Damn it, Payton."

"I needed to make sure. Before you knew about the baby."

"Why? So you could back yourself into a corner you can't get out of? Well, forget it. Forget what I said and forget about not marrying me. Everything's different now."

"Not everything." Their eyes clashed, held. Hers telling him she wouldn't back down. His begging to differ.

"You aren't thinking straight," he said levelly, his body language conveying all the confidence in the world that she'd see it his way. But she was onto his manipulative tactics.

Fat chance.

"You're a smart woman. All you need is some rest and a little perspective in the morning. We'll get you something to eat. Do you have any cravings? I'll have anything you want here inside thirty minutes."

"Nate, stop—"

"*No.* We'll get you some dinner and we'll go to bed. With you in my arms…and our baby inside you."

Her breath caught as a wave of emotion crashed through her, so intense her throat seized and her vision swam. And like that, the bliss of numb was torn away, leaving her raw and trembling. "I said stop!"

"I'm not stopping!" he snapped, those blue eyes she'd once been foolish enough to call arctic blazing at her. "Not until you see reason on this."

"Reason?" She was on her feet then, glaring at him across the table. "Give me a break. You go from assuring me there's *no chance* for a future with us to offering up the rest of your life—complete with a gold band and handy prenup—within the span of thirty minutes. Who's not being reasonable?"

"We're going to have a baby. A child between us. It changes things. I'm adapting."

"Then you better find another way to do it, Nate, because I'm not marrying you. There's no love—no emotion behind your proposal and I don't want to live the rest of my life as an obligation."

"That's not how it would be." A harsh breath followed as he threw one hand up in question. "I don't see why you're fighting this. *You're getting what you wanted*."

"Like hell I am!" How could he even think that?

He watched her. Waited a beat as though assessing the situation before replying. Slowly, so she wouldn't miss even one word. "*Like hell you won't*. I'll make you happy. You know I can." The muscle in his jaw jumped. "You said it yourself—we get along great together. We have fun."

"I want more than fun, Nate."

Exasperation shot up his brows. "And I'm offering it."

Not even close. "Can you deny that an hour ago the idea of this future you're asking me to share with you didn't have you running in the other direction?"

"An hour ago I thought I had a choice!"

Mistake. Payton's frame shook as though he'd struck her.

Too late, he saw his error. Damn it, he was blowing this, but she wasn't giving in!

"I'm sorry." Rounding the table, he pulled her into his arms and shifted them both back into the chair so she rested in his lap. "That's not what I meant."

"Yes, it is," she whispered, pressing her face into his chest so her soft curls spilled over him.

His arms tightened over shoulders that had never seemed so slight before. The hammering in his chest eased and for a moment they sat quietly together. And then she drew back, peering up at him, with those big brown eyes, liquid and pleading. "Nate, can't you understand that I don't want to take a lifetime of choices from you? That maybe I don't want you to take them from me?"

He understood it, all right. And was more sorry than he could have imagined possible. He knew what she was going through. Knew the feeling of betrayal that had to be welling inside of her. He'd tasted that bitterness, knew firsthand the threat of someone taking the life he'd planned. Only this time, Nate's carelessness had been the culprit to take Payton's choices and no test six months from now could set her free.

Damn it, he hadn't wanted to take anything away from her. It was the reason he ended things between them. He'd wanted her to be able to move on and find the man who would care for her the way she needed, wholly, without reservation. Only with those two uttered words, "I'm pregnant," that man became him.

Unlike with Annegret, there wasn't a single doubt in his mind. This baby was his—which meant so was Payton. And getting her to accept that was the first priority.

Fundamentally, he understood the problem. Payton had had a mere handful of hours to come to terms with the fact her life had changed immediately and irrevocably. Whereas, he'd been through this before—had months to contemplate his sense of priorities and values as they applied to a child entering his life. He'd known then what he would do, as he knew now.

He'd make a family. Make them whole.

"I understand, Payton. I do. But everything is different now that there's a baby. We're bound together for the rest of our lives through the child inside you."

"I'm not arguing that, but it doesn't mean we have to get married. You know I would never keep you from seeing him."

Him. She thought it would be a boy. He closed his eyes, pushing back the images that one word conjured. Visions he wasn't yet ready to face. "No. You won't. Because we'll be together. All of us."

She tried to stand, but he held her in place. Close to him, where she belonged.

"Nate, what you're suggesting is—"

"Important."

"Impossible. There are all kinds of families. People with situations much more convoluted than ours make it work without being married."

He shook his head, cupped her chin in his palm. "It won't work for me if I miss out on half of my child's life because I don't live with him."

Payton wanted to shove against his chest and scream her frustration, but the stress of the day had taken its toll and sapped the little energy she'd begun with. Now all she could do was whisper her protest. "I can't."

"I know you're scared, sweetheart. But I swear you don't have to be. We'll work this out. It doesn't have to happen tonight."

"No. It doesn't." They both needed some time to get used to the idea. Figure out how they really felt. What they wanted.

Nate would see.

"Have you told anyone yet?"

She shook her head. "No. Not yet."

"I'd appreciate it if you didn't. Not for a while."

She pulled back, searching his face for some sign of why, but all she saw was a man closed down and unavailable to her.

A sudden anxiety rose within her. Had he started to see someone else? Her stomach hollowed. Was there a woman he needed to tell? To give up—

"My dad. After what happened with Annegret—all the uncertainty. I'd rather wait to tell him about the pregnancy until we've sorted more of the details out ourselves."

His father. She should have realized.

"Of course. I won't say anything," she promised, the threat of tears leaving her voice unsteady.

Why couldn't he just love her? Why couldn't he have told her there was a chance for them? That walking away from what they'd had was tearing him apart? Given her *anything* to pin her hopes on so now she could take his reassurances and promises and wrap herself tight in them. Why did she have to know that an hour ago he still hadn't wanted her?

To that last, she reminded herself the answer was simple. She'd made him tell her. Because signing on to a loveless marriage wasn't something she could live with. Or perhaps it was. But a marriage where *she loved Nate* and he didn't love her? No. That would be a daily heartbreak she couldn't endure. So she'd demanded the truth.

Nate's wide hand gathered her hair at the nape of her neck, stroked over the mass of it as he pulled her close. "We'll work it out, sweetheart. I promise."

Too weary to do anything else, she gave into the comfort of a hold she'd never wanted to give up—from a man who didn't love her.

CHAPTER TWENTY-TWO

How in the hell was he supposed to make this work when Payton wouldn't give a damn inch?

"I'm not giving up my job!" Her cheeks were flush, her eyes overbright with shadows beneath as she planted hands on hips and glared at him from across the distance of his living room.

"People work because they need the money," he answered steadily, unwilling to be baited into a shouting match with this stubborn little demon woman carrying his child. "*You* don't need the money." He was the calm one. The reasonable one. Casually sprawled in his chair, smiling his most patient, unfazed smile—his hand, all the while, discreetly flexing the tension from his body behind the arm of the wingback.

They'd been going round like this for an hour now. And engaging in some variation of it for a month. He'd make a suggestion. She'd take offense. He'd clarify, take a different tack. She'd glower and throw whatever he'd offered back in his face. It didn't matter what merit his idea held. If the suggestion came from him, she didn't trust it, assuming it tied into his grand scheme to get her married to him.

She was right.

"Really, Nate? How do you feel about charity? How did you feel about it back when you weren't the one offering?"

He took a steadying breath. "Payton, this isn't charity.

There are laws in place to ensure that fathers provide for their children. I'm providing."

Her eyes flashed accusation. "You're trying to make me dependent on you."

"That isn't true. While the idea of taking care of you appeals to me a great deal, stealing your independence is not my goal here." He pushed up from the chair and paced between the fireplace and the bank of windows fronting the apartment. Blazing to bleak and back again. There was no good place to be.

"Hell, Payton, I'm not a villain. I want to make sure you and our baby have everything. I don't want you to work when you're tired. I don't want you to have to leave our child with a nanny because you can't afford not to. Can't you see I want to help here?" *And help my cause by offering assistance as I remind you of the practicalities surrounding a single mother's life.*

"I don't want any help." But even as she said the words the glitter of coming tears filled her eyes. She was scared and, though he'd been there every step of the way, he knew she felt alone. Because every step of the way, he'd been coming at her, working his own agenda. Trying to break her down enough that she'd let him pick her up.

A tremble touched her lips.

Why wouldn't she just *give*?

He was sick of the adversarial tango between them. He could barely remember what it had been like between them before they'd found out about the baby— No. That wasn't true. It would be easier if he could forget because he missed what they'd had. Missed the laughter and softness. The thoughtful exchanges. The hot rush that surged through him when that wild smile burst across her lips. He missed her body. Her heart. The show of too much emotion shining in her eyes when she was beneath him—that had been damn near impossible to give up. He wanted it back. Wanted to grab her shoulders and shake until she saw sense, stopped being so bullheaded and took the life he was offering her.

Watching him with wary eyes, she let out a defeated sigh and turned, giving him her back.

Screw this.

He had months before the baby came—before he *had* to get his shackle around her ring finger. Yes, he wanted resolution sooner. Like last week. But today he wasn't getting anywhere. Payton needed comfort, and he'd be damned if he wasn't going to lend her some.

Ignoring the aching memory of her eager acceptance of his hold—that perfect fit—he pulled Payton's tension-stiff frame into his arms and didn't let go. He stroked a hand down her back, bent his head to hers, and whispered into her hair. "Payton, stop fighting me. I know you're upset and we don't see eye to eye on…most anything these days. But this is new for us both. We're going to figure it out together. Okay?"

Her body shuddered once, and then she gave in. Softening against him as the tension sapped from her frame. "I'm going crazy, Nate. I'm so upset. And I—I—"

"Shh. I'll be there for you," he promised. "Both of you. No matter what."

Her head bowed forward, the crown rubbing against the center of his chest as she succumbed to a quiet sob.

Ducking to the side, he caught her against him, sweeping an arm beneath her knees. She didn't fight him as he carried her to the corner of the couch closest to the fire and held her in his lap as her tears soaked his shirt.

He'd take care of her. Whether she wanted him to or not, he'd make her happy. She just had to stop fighting him first.

She'd fallen asleep. It was a mistake, but curled in the strength of Nate's arms she'd felt so safe and calm and she'd been so tired…and then she'd let go. Let fatigue take her. Only now she wasn't tired. But she was still folded into his lap, enveloped in his clean masculine scent, closer than she'd been to him in a month, compounding her mistake with each breath drawn and every passing second she lingered.

Tilting her head, she peered up to his sleeping face. The lines of strain around his eyes, recently etched so deep, were softened and smoothed. His mouth relaxed into the near-smile that was its natural state.

A heavy breath filled the chest beneath her, followed by the rough growl of Nate waking. God, she loved that sound.

He was offering her a lifetime of hearing it. A lifetime of mornings waking to the hard-hewn planes of his face, the security of his arms.

He surveyed her through half-lidded eyes, a slow curve touching his lips before his focus sharpened on her. Heated.

She knew what that steam-rising, jungle gaze meant. *Trouble*.

She tried to pull back, but couldn't—literally.

"Oh!" Her hair tugged against the buttons of the oxford she'd been crashed out on.

Nate shifted up, only minimally pulling at the caught hair. "Hold on, sweetheart. Let me—"

"Ouch!"

"Sorry, whoa, stop squirming."

Keenly aware of her positioning, Payton stilled, her fingers attempting to pull the loose strands from the caught batch. But Nate brushed her hand away.

"Just give me a second." He reached to his back and pulled the shirt over his head, careful to keep the snagged buttons in one place. And then she was free. Sort of. Free from being physically attached to Nate's chest. Only her hair, falling in a tangled curtain in front of her eyes, was still wound up in his buttons. And she was still sitting in his lap.

"Okay, I see it here."

Good. She couldn't see a thing.

Long fingers sifted through the heavy mass, sending shivers of pleasure coursing over her skin.

Not good.

"I can get it." She reached out a staying hand, only to retract it with a jerk when she encountered warm, hard flesh. Nate. Bare-chested and less than six inches away.

"Probably not without scissors. I can see what I'm doing, just hold still."

Another gentle tug and the shirt partially fell away. "That's one."

"What?" she squeaked.

"You're snagged on two here. Probably that little nuzzling thing you do when you're asleep. I guess I must've been shirtless all the other times."

Her mouth went dry. As he was shirtless now. She let out a slow breath and closed her eyes, only to find the stimulus of his touch intensified—his hand sifting gently through her hair, readjusting, gathering, gripping tight and then gentling again—

The shirt came free and she thought she'd been spared, except when Nate tossed it aside she could see what had been opposite that soft button-down— Bare skin and hard-packed muscle. The perfect tight discs of his nipples. The fine line of hair bisecting his torso, trailing into his pants and flaring wide across his pecs. All of it flickering golden in the dying firelight.

She swallowed, raising her eyes to meet the blue of Nate's—steadily fixed on her. A muscle twitched in his jaw.

"Thank you," she whispered, backing off his lap, her gaze dropping to his chest once more as she stepped free.

He didn't answer, just sat there, brows drawn down, watching as she silently collected her things. At the door she turned

to him, seeing the man she'd fallen in love with staring back at
her for the first time in a month. No antagonism. No calculating manipulation. Just Nate. Wanting her.

She pushed a tremulous smile to her lips. "I'll talk to you
tomorrow." And then she fled.

At the snick of the door closing, Nate shoved off the couch
with a violent curse.

How the hell could he have been so blind? So stupid!

He'd been going about this all wrong. Wasting precious
time respecting Payton's boundaries. Believing the physical
interaction—always so easy between them—had become a
necessary casualty in his pursuit of her hand. Like an idiot,
he'd kept his distance, waiting for her to realize that marrying
him was her best option before revisiting the sexual chem-
istry between them. But that had been backwards thinking,
and all it had won him was a month of frustrated nights and
the woman he wanted getting too damn comfortable with an
arm's length space-cushion.

What he'd just seen—that smolder of lust banked not quite
well enough—told him he didn't need space or understanding.
He needed seduction. Dirty, down-low seduction that would
get Payton writhing, naked beneath him.

The sex had always been more emotional than she'd wanted
to admit. He'd known it from the start. Even that first night,
he'd seen it in her eyes. She couldn't leave her heart out of
anything she did, least of all making love.

So he needed to get her back into his bed. Use his body
to batter down her defenses. Unlock the emotions and wants
she'd tried to banish. And once he got her there, made her
moan and gasp and look up at him with those eyes that gave
too much away, he'd hold on and wouldn't let go. He'd make
her feel so good she wouldn't think twice when they hopped
on a plane to Vegas.

And that was how it was going to have to go. Fast. No time

for second thoughts or backtracking. The only problem was actually getting her beneath him.

If she saw him coming, she'd shut him down a mile away.

So the trick would be to exploit her weakness without letting on what he was doing. Based on the way their proximity and his state of undress affected her tonight, he had a good idea of where to start.

It wasn't fair play, but playing fair hadn't gotten him where he needed to go. He wanted her back. Wanted this whole matter resolved. Payton in his bed. His ring on her finger. Their baby between them.

And now he had a plan.

CHAPTER TWENTY-THREE

PAYTON stood before the closed door to her apartment, hand hovering above the knob as she mentally shored up her defenses. Nate was on his way up. Invariably looking like a new page in some man-by-month calendar, and too dangerously good for her peace of mind. He always looked good. And she'd generally been able to handle it. Register the attraction, tamp it down, sweep it aside. Right up until the night a week ago when she'd gotten her hair stuck in his shirt. Ever since she'd been fighting a losing battle against temptation.

It was unsettling. And what made matters worse, Nate had stopped berating her with the merits of marriage. Oh, she wanted to believe he'd suddenly come to terms with the impossibility of that scenario for her, but this was *Nate*. Relentless. Ruthless. Single-minded in his unwavering determination to make the world bend to his will, Nate. Now that she'd been on the receiving end of all that intensive focus, she didn't believe for one minute he'd actually given up the fight.

Which meant he'd be coming at her in some new devious manner. Unless of course the hormones had made her paranoid in addition to everything else: Hungry, sick, weepy, tired, irritable, sentimental…the list went on and on.

"Hey, Payton, you planning to let me in?"

Startled, she grabbed for the knob, shaking off her suspicion in the hopes of spending a pleasant morning with the father of her child. Whether his change in attitude was legitimate or not, she couldn't deny that Nate in "friend" mode was far superior to Nate as "adversary".

Swinging the door open, an apology poised on her lips, she stared in stunned disbelief…at her high-school fantasy come to life.

Nate Evans dressed in black soccer shorts, jersey, guards and cleats, a ball tucked under his arm and a sport bag slung over his shoulder.

Oh…my…

"I know we'd talked about looking into those Lamaze classes, but Rafe needed a fill-in for this morning's game." One shoulder propped against the doorjamb, not really in or out, he cocked his head toward the hall. "Wondered if you'd like to put the research off until afternoon and get out for some fresh air now?"

She swallowed, trying to loosen her throat enough to spit out a simple, smart, "No, thank you". Only she truly loved soccer. It had been ages since she'd seen a game and, as she remembered it, there wasn't much better than watching Nate play. Besides, he was right, it was a beautiful day—crisp and sunny, in the low fifties. She'd been planning a walk down at the lakefront anyway so it didn't make sense not to go just because her libido had all but rolled over to beg at the sight of Nate outfitted in soccer gear.

God help her, what was she going to do?

Forty minutes later, Payton was comfortably situated in a folding chair Nate had dragged out of the trunk of his car. She had a bottle of water, an organic green apple and a clear view of the players warming up before the game. Nate juggled the ball a few times, causing her gaze to drift down to his legs, the heavy muscles of his thighs flexing and bunching as he deftly passed the ball from knee to knee and then caught it in his hands and brought it back to his chest.

Those legs. Her mouth watered…

What was she doing? The days of pining were over. She wasn't waiting for her favorite player to notice her anymore. He'd noticed. Knocked her up and thrown her over already. Now the only game she could afford to play was keep away. And mooning over the silky caress of his shorts as he limbered up his legs was a definite violation of the rules.

So why then, minutes later, when he scored his first goal and shot her one of those victorious smiles that never ceased to devastate her heart, was she jumping from her seat cheering with the unrestrained enthusiasm of a fourteen-year-old girl dreaming of love and happily-ever-after?

Two things not on offer.

With that in mind, she tempered her reaction and returned to her seat. Forced the cool reserve she'd long ago perfected and watched Nate tear down the field. Held steady when she caught the flinty shift in his eyes.

He was assessing. Calculating. Strategizing for a tactical advantage in a game that had nothing to do with landing a ball in the goal.

He was playing her.

Driving forward, circling back and taking shot after shot until he found a way to outmaneuver her defense. He wanted the win. Her and the baby under his roof and in his care. He wanted to do the "right thing", only he couldn't seem to grasp how *not right* living that life would be for any of them.

Nate said he didn't want their child to miss out on the full-time love and attention living with both of its parents would afford. But what he wasn't considering were the implications of growing up in an environment of pretend. Children knew. Though they might not be able to discern the complexities of why, they sensed when something in their home was off. Like an imbalance of power or detachment of emotion.

Nate had never wanted to marry her. He'd never wanted

a child. And though he said all the right things, talked such a good game about raising their baby, she'd yet to see any indication from him that the child growing inside of her was more than something to claim. He knew it was there. He knew how fathers were *supposed* to feel. What they were supposed to do. But he didn't actually have those feelings himself. And no matter how he might want to provide a perfect life, no one could convincingly fake an attachment they didn't feel forever, something Nate knew from firsthand experience.

Add to that a mother's heartbreak made new through each passing day of make-believe affection—what kind of life would that be for their child?

The kind she didn't want to imagine and wouldn't allow to come to pass. She couldn't make Nate feel. She couldn't make him love. But she could ensure that her child always had a safe haven to return to. A place where the love was unconditional and abundant and the emotional stability wouldn't waiver.

She could do it. So long as she remembered that marrying Nate was not an option.

The game had been fast paced and exciting. The teams evenly matched, exactly the kind of challenge Nate thrived on. But the thrill of the win was dampened by the loss of ground he couldn't explain, except to say, one minute he'd had Payton looking at him as she had all those years before. And the next she'd closed down. Shuttered her emotions and put all that distance back between them.

Unwilling to concede any form of defeat, he jogged over to where she stood at the sidelines, blanket and chair clutched in her arms like a shield—against him.

Going to take more than that, sweetheart.

Giving her his grin, he grabbed her load and tucked it under one arm.

She blinked, looking just nervous enough to truly whet his appetite.

Go ahead and run. Try it.

"So congratulations," she said with a timid wave toward the field behind them.

"Yeah, good game, wasn't it?" He wiped the sweat from his brow with a sweep of his forearm, and caught the hungry drift of her gaze following his motions.

"You were terrific."

"It felt good to get on the field again." Have an outlet for some of the tension accumulated over the last month. Though as outlets went, he had a better one in mind. One he intended to make use of before the day's end.

Suddenly he couldn't wait to get back to Payton's place and put his plan into action. He ducked down to grab his athletic bag, straightened and then froze as the dark brown eyes he always thought of as soft and vulnerable bore straight into him—cold and hard.

He didn't like it. She was thinking too much.

But he knew exactly how to make her stop.

Looking away, he hiked the bag over a shoulder. "Let's get out of here."

The ride back into the city took longer than he'd liked. Too much time for Payton to sit quietly, contemplating her defensive strategies. He'd kept up the conversation, but her head hadn't been in it and eventually he'd left her to her thoughts.

At the apartment she'd predictably tried to put him off about the afternoon, but he had the Lamaze research as his passport and easily gained entry. From there, it was just a matter of chipping away her defenses...one garment at a time. He wished he'd had a camera for the way her jaw dropped when he jerked his jersey over his head—outwardly oblivious to the impact of his actions, inwardly gloating over her reaction to his unsubtle striptease.

And how could she argue when he suggested they look over the different schedules and programs…after he'd cleaned up in the shower? By the time he'd headed off to her bathroom, she'd been shaking, unable to even look at him.

Perfect. And that was just the warm up.

This was the main event. Nate glared into the fogged mirror. It was go time.

"Hey, babe?" Nate called from down the hall.

Payton looked up from the magazine she'd been blindly staring at for the last ten minutes while futilely attempting to keep her mind out of the shower where all that lathering was taking place. Talk about wasted effort. Try as she might to stop them, images of slow-running suds slipping over hard-packed muscles, tight nipples and more flitted one after the next through her mind. Memories of the salty taste of his skin… Not good.

With a shake of her head, she stood, calling back, "Wha—?" but that was as far as she got.

"Did I leave my bag out here?" Nate stood in the hall, a white towel hanging precariously low on his hips. He smiled crookedly her way while he used another towel to rub his hair dry.

The air in her lungs leaked out in a slow hiss, leaving her empty and weak, stunned and lightheaded, hungry and horrified as she fell back into her seat.

The crooked smile vanished, pulling into a hard frown as he dropped to a knee at her side. Concern furrowed his brow. Concern and something else she couldn't quite—

"Payton, sweetheart, are you okay?"

"Yes—no," she stammered in confusion, her chin tucking back. "I'm fine…" But then he was right there. So close she could feel the damp heat rising off his skin, see the water beaded across his chest and shoulders, his eyelashes clinging together in darkened points that made the blue of his eyes stand out bright in vivid contrast.

"You're pale." His voice was a low rumble at her ear, rough and midnight dark in the middle of the day. And then his big hands were moving over her, checking, gently probing... touching her in a way she knew she should stop but couldn't summon the strength to do so. "No swollen glands."

"Nate." Her voice was weak, thready. Something even she wouldn't listen to.

Long fingers skimmed up her neck, teasing through the hairs at her nape... "Chills." They curled over her jaw, brushed her cheeks, and then moved in a slow caress to her forehead. "Flushed, but not feverish."

His thumb swept a gentle arc across her cheekbone as his gaze locked with hers, pulling in slow strokes at that secret place where all her dreams dwelled.

Tell me. Tell me you love me. Give me something. Anything.

"Your pupils are dilated," he murmured. But there was nothing wrong with her. Nothing beyond the fact that temptation had just taken her a step closer to ruin. Making her pulse race and the air go thin and her body begin its achy plea for more of the touch she'd gone too long without.

She wanted him. Needed him. And if it were only her—but it wasn't.

She swallowed. Closed her eyes and thought about her baby before opening them again. "My eyes are fine, Nate." She'd be fine if he stopped touching her.

"Then what is it?" he challenged, meeting her gaze head-on, the heat of it stoking her to smolder.

Tell him. Only if she said the words, let him know how seeing him like this affected her, then he'd use it against—

Wait. The bag in the hall? He couldn't. The shower. The striptease complete with the stretching-out of all those muscles. He wouldn't dare! Only, this was Nate and he'd decided what he wanted. To hell with everyone else.

The soccer game! How long? This week for sure. Her stomach sank with dread.

Heat flamed her skin, only it had nothing to do with attraction and everything to do with outrage.

So he thought he could play her by using his body? Well, she knew a thing about that game. She knew what he liked, knew what sent him past the brink of control. And he'd just given her a lesson in how to achieve it without investing any actual emotion. Thank you, Nate. She could do that, too.

Time for Nate Evans to get a taste of his own medicine.

CHAPTER TWENTY-FOUR

He was losing her.

He'd been so close. She'd been there, he knew it. He'd seen her weaken, start to melt. Felt the hot lick of her eyes over his skin, the current charging the air between them. And then, just that quickly, it changed.

The temperature dropped. The static grounded. And a swarm of angry bees manifested beneath his skin, buzzing in his head, making him itch and sting and want to roar in painful frustration.

Why wouldn't she damned well *give*?

Fighting the vise around his chest, he surged to his feet. Wasn't surprised when Payton rose with him. She leaned into his space, looking up at him with eyes that were flat and bleak, devoid of emotion and speared through his soul like a blade.

"Maybe I don't feel so well after all." Her hand settled cold at the center of his chest.

No. He saw what she was offering him—nothing—and he wouldn't take it.

He wouldn't let her look at him like that. As if somehow the lively, soulful woman who'd lived in this body had been obliterated, leaving an empty husk behind. No, not empty. Just unavailable to him. He couldn't stand it. Wouldn't allow it. Wouldn't let her shut him out and look through him as if he weren't even there.

With too much testosterone burning through his veins like acid, his hands moved possessively to Payton's hips. His thumbs rubbing deliberately over the delicate bones there.

He knew her and no matter how she wanted to close down and bury herself away from him, she couldn't do it completely. But if he wanted her, alive and hot and angry in his arms, he had to find the spot where she was most vulnerable and—even if it meant he was going straight to hell for it—cut deep.

Gaze fixed on the opaque waters of her eyes, he skimmed a hand beneath the hem of her shirt at her hip. Took a gulp of air and braced every muscle in his body as he pressed his palm to the one spot he hadn't touched—hadn't wanted to touch—in all the weeks since he'd learned about the pregnancy.

Payton flinched, her eyes going wide and sparking with all the emotion she'd wanted to cloak. Rage and hurt flashed beneath the surface. And then something stronger than them both swirled in the liquid brown depths below. Hope. The sight of it was so powerfully alluring after the bleakness he'd witnessed only seconds ago, he didn't know if he could ever break free from its spell.

If he ever wanted to.

But then Payton's hands covered his own where they lay flat against her belly—and the world tilted off its axis as they held their child together for the very first time.

There was a soft rise to the belly that had been a flat plane the last time he'd laid his hand to it. A gentle mound protecting the tiny body within. His child. The mergence of two souls into one. *Their child*.

He swallowed, unable to speak. And suddenly he was on his knees, pushing her shirt at both sides so he could see. So he could feel.

His thumbs brushed the smooth skin around her navel.

And then he pressed his forehead against the softness there, turned his ear to rest against her. Wondering if he could hear the sound of her body building its precious shelter. If his baby could hear him.

"Hello?" he whispered against her skin, unable to stop himself.

Slight fingers stroked his hair, teasing through the strands with that familiar touch that after too long without had become foreign.

He turned into her belly and kissed. Drew in the sweet perfume of her skin and kissed again, opening his mouth against her as he prayed she wouldn't push him away. Wouldn't close herself off to him. Again and again, he kissed across the feminine terrain until Payton's fingers tightened in his hair, holding him close.

One thought repeating through his mind. A primal claim, sounding to the rhythm of his pounding heart.

Mine. Mine. Mine.

They both were. And in a way he never could have predicted. Straight through to his soul.

It terrified him. Made his pulse race faster and his hands clutch at the woman he hadn't known how to hold.

Except she was letting him hold her now. Giving him the gift of her body, if only for this one time.

He couldn't think about that. Couldn't think about the void in her eyes when she'd uncovered his latest manipulation. He never wanted to see that look again. Didn't want to think about what it meant that after all the years, he had been the one to put it there. Didn't want to think about what it would take to ensure it never happened again.

Payton knew better. Knew she was headed for heartbreak, but still couldn't back away. A moment before she'd been at the brink of resisting, and then she'd seen it. The instant Nate's universe changed, taking the man she loved to his knees. The look in his eyes when his hand touched her belly. The sense of marvel. Wonder. He'd cradled their child in the palm of his hand. Kissed the place where it grew within her.

The tenderness of that kiss would stay with her for the rest of her life.

There was no more fight. No more will. Only want and the desperate need to give in. Give herself over.

He didn't love her. Maybe he couldn't. But he loved their baby and she didn't have to worry for her child's sake. In that instant she'd seen Nate's father in his eyes. The love and devotion apparent to anyone who crossed their paths. And she knew with sudden vivid clarity that she couldn't deny them a single moment together.

It would be enough for her. More than enough.

Her fingers trembled as they touched his jaw in silent inquiry. He turned up to her, the stark need and depth of emotion in his eyes taking her breath away.

"Let me have you."

She nodded, unable to voice even the most simple word of acceptance.

Nate rose then, so tall and powerful before her. His muscles standing out as though each and every one had gone taut beneath the strain of the last hour.

She reached for the towel at his waist, her fingers trembling as she loosened the cinch. Let it fall away and then grasped the hem of her own shirt.

Nate watched with hungry eyes as she pulled the stretchy cotton overhead and then opened the front catch to her newly too-tight bra. Her breasts spilled free, and she saw that single telling vein pop to life, betraying the expense of his restraint. Restraint she understood was meant to show her he would not take. This time he would wait for her to give.

Her thumbs slipped into the waist of her yoga pants and panties. She pushed them down her hips. Let them pile at her feet before she stepped free, as naked and exposed as the man who waited for her with a single outstretched arm.

He took her into his embrace, wrapping his long arms around her in a hold so flawless it made her ache. She didn't know how long he would have held her that way, but he was thick and hard against her belly, his perfect beaded nipple a scant distance from her mouth, close enough to touch with the barest flick of her tongue. She couldn't help herself.

And all that tightly reined restraint snapped.

Nate swept her into his arms, a gruff sound grating from his throat as she opened beneath the fall of his kiss. Took the thrust of his tongue and twisted in his arms to press her breasts against the harsh rise and fall of his chest.

In her bedroom, Nate propped a knee at the mattress, setting her back with a careful precision—so different from the times he'd tossed her to his bed and followed her down, laughing and growling as he crawled up her body to claim her. This wasn't playful. It wasn't fun.

It was undiluted desperation to join as one.

Mouths fused, tongues mating, sliding over and around each other as their bodies aligned in all the right places. Nate poised at the opening of her body, held back, gritting his teeth against his need to sink deep. Take. Claim. Keep.

Payton peered up at him, her eyes smoked with a need that matched his own, and yet she, too, paused. Her hand cupped his cheek. "I can't fight anymore."

"No more." His voice was a broken rasp. "I promise." He'd glimpsed what it would look like to destroy the only thing he had worth fighting for, and he wouldn't risk it again.

Her body arched against him, wet and too inviting to resist. "Nate, please. Now."

He pushed inside then, groaning as he sank full length into her tight hold. Gritting his teeth through the pure skin-to-skin friction.

Heaven.

To be so close.

To be let in.

To be *together*.

It was physical pleasure, but so much more than that and he never wanted it to end.

He arched back, sank deep again, drawing out each long stroke as far as it would go. Savoring the hug of Payton's legs around his hips, her fingers in his hair holding him close. The breathy pants of her rising desire. The clutch of her body when she took the kiss of his groin against hers. The escalating cries and pleas for more. He wanted to give her more. Give her everything. All he had and all he was. Anything she asked so he never lost this again.

And when her lips parted on a silent cry, her body seized around him, and she stared up at him with those soulful brown eyes that begged him to hold her…longer…harder…just like that…daring him to make it last forever—the world shifted again and he knew it would never be the same.

Braced on strong arms above her, Nate searched her eyes, his deep blue stare more penetrating than the hard body that rocked within her own. He carried her through the crashing waves of orgasm, followed the receding tide, and then urged her into the surf again. Not once looking away.

Let him see.

I love you.

He knew already.

Always you.

There was nothing left to hide.

Forever you.

He drove hard inside her. She arched against him, reveling in the stretch and give of her body as he filled her again and again, taking her fast toward the peak from which she'd just returned.

"Don't stop, please," she gasped, clutching tight at his shoulders. "Please."

He gathered her closer, slid an arm beneath her hips and held her to him as his voice rasped over her soul. "Just let me love you."

She cried out, her body pushed to release. Her heart torn in two. The world shattering around them as Nate followed her over the edge, her name on his lips.

Then gasping ragged breaths, he rolled to her side keeping one arm slung across her waist as he pulled her into the warmth of his body. She buried her face in his chest, letting the moments pass until Nate slipped into an oblivion beyond her grasp.

"Just let me love you."

They were beautiful words of passion to describe the physical act. So beautiful she could almost pretend…

CHAPTER TWENTY-FIVE

NATE sat at the edge of the bed, feet on the floor, forearms propped over his knees, jaw painfully set.

This wasn't going to work.

He looked over his shoulder at Payton's sleeping form, quietly curled into herself, a tiny furrow pulled between her delicate brows.

She didn't want what he was offering. Not really. They'd been in the same book, but on different pages from the start. He'd tried not to hurt her, but he'd been an idiot and in the end that was all he'd managed to do. Even today, when suddenly all the pieces of his life seemed to be falling into place, one jagged edge didn't fit and he'd felt it cut through Payton's vulnerable heart.

Just let me love you.

He shouldn't have said the words like that. What the hell had he been thinking?

Dropping his head into his hands, he let out a frustrated growl. A small noise of protest sounded from behind him as Payton clutched the corner of the sheet closer to her. She needed to rest. Needed a break. Needed a hell of a lot better than what he'd been giving her.

He knew what he had to do.

He pushed to his feet and found the comforter on the floor at the far corner of the bed. Covered her with it and quietly left.

* * *

The afternoon light was dying, leaving puddles of amber and burnt sienna across the western sky. Payton stood by the window, her forehead pressed to the glass, Nate's note in hand. She'd found it on the kitchen table after waking to an empty bed and quiet apartment a half-hour before. Had stalled in her steps at the sight of the single sheet propped against the bud-vase—inexplicably terrified. But the note had been no more than to tell her he'd had a few things to take care of and would be back later. Nothing earth-shattering or cryptic or telling. A few lines about some errands.

She needed to stop being so dramatic.

At the sound of the lock tumbling from down the hall, she straightened. Set the note on the counter and headed toward the door where Nate had just walked in, burdened with an overflowing grocery bag.

Food, she realized with a smile. The man was forever trying to take care of her. Tonight he wanted to make sure she ate a healthy meal.

"Sorry I was gone so long," he apologized, dropping a kiss at her temple before carrying the groceries through to the kitchen. "I stopped to pick up some dinner on the way back."

On the way back? "Were you at the office?"

He set the bag on the counter and turned to her, those too-blue eyes so beautiful they made her weak. "I drove out to my dad's."

"Did you tell him…about the baby?" About them? He'd been waiting to tell his father, she knew, until he'd gotten a marriage commitment from her.

Nate nodded.

So he'd read her decision in her eyes. Just as well. No need to make a big production of telling him he'd won.

No. That wasn't right. It stopped being a game the moment

she'd seen his eyes fill with love for their child. No more fighting. No winners. No losers.

Abandoning the food, he took her into his arms. He smelled so good and felt so strong around her. She'd have this for the rest of her life.

"I told him you were pregnant. And that we weren't getting married."

It took a moment for the words to make sense. She pushed back and looked up into his eyes, stunned. Shocked. And scared.

Her throat was tight and her knees loose. "What—why—?"

She didn't understand. Couldn't form the words to ask for clarification, explanation.

Nate's head dropped, his mouth pulling into a pained grimace. "I've been such a bastard. I never wanted to hurt you. But I've been doing it for so long now I can't remember a time when I wasn't."

She remembered. Her hand pressed flat to his chest, resting over the heavy thump, thump of his heart. "Things have been hard over the last months. Everything changed in the blink of an eye and we've both been reacting emotionally."

"No. That's just it. I haven't been. If I'd been in touch with anything beyond my need to control the situation, I would have realized that forcing you into a loveless marriage wouldn't be fair to either of us."

The words stung, sliced through her, cutting deep. He was giving her what she'd wanted. Wasn't he? Suddenly it didn't feel like it. It felt as if the ground were giving way beneath her feet and she were losing everything.

Forcing herself to nod, she pushed the barest smile to her lips. "How did your father take the news?"

Nate let out a self-deprecating laugh. "He was annoyed I'd waited this long to tell him."

"I bet." She'd known it was hard on him to keep the secret. But he hadn't been ready.

"He was happy to hear I was making him a grandfather, even if I wasn't making an honest woman of you." He shoved a hand through the short waves of his hair, ran it over the muscles of his neck. "But he agreed that after the horse's ass I've been, I was going to lose you forever if I kept pushing you to marry me."

She blinked up at him, to find those blue, blue eyes fixed intently on her. "What are you saying?"

"Payton, I've been such an idiot. I pushed you away, thinking you deserved more than I could give. It was the hardest thing I'd ever done, but I wanted you to have everything—love, marriage, family—all the things I didn't believe I was capable of sharing with you. And then I found out you were pregnant. Without having to examine why I needed it so badly, I suddenly had my justification to hold onto you forever. Only I was so intent on tying you down and fitting us into this perfect box, I didn't realize I'd been backing you into a prison."

Her mouth opened and then snapped closed at the realization she had no idea what to say to him. He finally understood, but how could she explain that when he knocked down the walls and took away the lock, that prison became paradise— the only place she wanted to live.

"I want us to be a family, Payton. But not because it's something I have to do. Not because it's a duty I feel honor bound to uphold. And sure as hell not for some paper certificate. I want it because I want you."

Tears of joy flooded her eyes. He hadn't offered her love, but he'd given her everything else she could ever want. It was enough. More than enough. "I want you, too. More than anything."

And then she was in his arms, held so hard against him. Safe and warm and basking in the promise of their future when the words she'd never thought to hear came gruff against the tumble of her curls. "I love you."

Payton pushed back from his hold, panic that she'd heard wrong or suddenly started hallucinating gripped her. Nate took a step back, letting her see him. The honesty of his words etched across the features of his beautiful face. Her heart tripped in her chest, and the room around her tilted and dimmed at the edges. She reached out grasping at air—found Nate's hand there to support her. She barely had the breath to ask, "You love me?"

"I really do. I didn't think I knew how. It was so foreign to me, so unfamiliar, I didn't recognize it even when it was shaking me to the core. Scaring the hell out of me." Those blue eyes stared steadily back at her, open, windows to a soul... brimming with hope. "I love you. And if you're willing to take a chance on me, I'll spend the rest of my life proving it to you."

Extracting a small black box from his back pocket, Nate went down on one knee. He flipped open the lid revealing an eternity band of glittering diamonds and held it out to her. "Payton Liss. I love you. Will you make me the happiest man alive by agreeing to live unwed with me for the duration of our lives? By allowing me to care for you, provide you with everything your heart desires, and love you and our baby forever?"

Her heart sped and helpless laughter bubbled free. He loved her!

She went to the floor beside him and, arms linking around his neck, answered, "No."

His head jerked up, a harsh bark of laughter escaping him. Amusement lit his eyes. That crazy confidence shining bright.

This man knew her. He really knew her.

"So after all that," he asked, voice thick with emotion he wouldn't hide, "now you want me to marry you, hmm?"

She peered up at him, letting him see everything her heart held. All the love. All the hope. Everything she knew he would cherish and protect. "I really do."

The corner of his mouth kicked into the grin she'd loved her whole life. "When?"

Pulling his head down to hers, she brushed her lips against his. Reveled in his tightening hold. "How fast can you make it happen?"

Before she could blink she'd been pulled into the cradle of his thighs, that gorgeous ring sparkled on her finger, and Nate was issuing orders into his phone.

"I want a plane for Vegas, ready to take off in one hour."

Nate pulled her closer and, holding the phone from his ear, stared deep into her eyes.

With one look, she told him everything he needed to know.

The muscle in his jaw jumped as his gaze went dark. "You're right. We better make it two."

Tossing the phone aside, he slid his fingers into the curls at her nape and captured her mouth with a kiss that touched her soul and tasted like forever.

Cupping her cheek in his palm, he brought his brow to hers. "Tell me. I need to hear the words."

"Forever, Nate. From so long ago and with everything I am. I love you. Always."

Coming Next Month

from **Harlequin Presents®**. Available January 25, 2011.

Coming Next Month

from **Harlequin Presents® EXTRA**. Available February 8, 2011.

HPECNM0111

REQUEST YOUR FREE BOOKS!

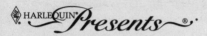 

2 FREE NOVELS PLUS
2 FREE GIFTS!

YES! Please send me 2 FREE Harlequin Presents® novels and my 2 FREE gifts (gifts are worth about $10). After receiving them, if I don't wish to receive any more books, I can return the shipping statement marked "cancel." If I don't cancel, I will receive 6 brand-new novels every month and be billed just $4.05 per book in the U.S. or $4.74 per book in Canada. That's a saving of at least 15% off the cover price! It's quite a bargain! Shipping and handling is just 50¢ per book.* I understand that accepting the 2 free books and gifts places me under no obligation to buy anything. I can always return a shipment and cancel at any time. Even if I never buy another book, the two free books and gifts are mine to keep forever.

106/306 HDN E5M4

Name	(PLEASE PRINT)	
Address		Apt. #
City	State/Prov.	Zip/Postal Code

Signature (if under 18, a parent or guardian must sign)

Mail to the **Harlequin Reader Service:**
IN U.S.A.: P.O. Box 1867, Buffalo, NY 14240-1867
IN CANADA: P.O. Box 609, Fort Erie, Ontario L2A 5X3

Not valid for current subscribers to Harlequin Presents books.

Are you a current subscriber to Harlequin Presents books and want to receive the larger-print edition? Call 1-800-873-8635 today!

* Terms and prices subject to change without notice. Prices do not include applicable taxes. N.Y. residents add applicable sales tax. Canadian residents will be charged applicable provincial taxes and GST. Offer not valid in Quebec. This offer is limited to one order per household. All orders subject to approval. Credit or debit balances in a customer's account(s) may be offset by any other outstanding balance owed by or to the customer. Please allow 4 to 6 weeks for delivery. Offer available while quantities last.

Your Privacy: Harlequin Books is committed to protecting your privacy. Our Privacy Policy is available online at www.eHarlequin.com or upon request from the Reader Service. From time to time we make our lists of customers available to reputable third parties who may have a product or service of interest to you. If you would prefer we not share your name and address, please check here. ☐

Help us get it right—We strive for accurate, respectful and relevant communications. To clarify or modify your communication preferences, visit us at www.ReaderService.com/consumerchoice.

HP10R

Harlequin Romance author Donna Alward is loved for her gorgeous rancher heroes.

Meet Wyatt as he's confronted by both a precious little pink bundle left on his doorstep and his neighbor Elli who's going to show him the ropes....

Introducing
PROUD RANCHER, PRECIOUS BUNDLE

THE SQUAWKING QUIETED as Elli picked the baby up, and Wyatt turned around, trying hard to ignore the feelings of inadequacy as Darcy immediately stopped fussing.

"Maybe she's uncomfortable. What do you think, sweetheart?" Elli turned her conversation to the baby.

"What do you think is wrong?" Wyatt asked, putting the coffee pot back on the burner.

A strange look passed over Elli's face, one that looked like guilt and panic. But it was gone quickly. "I couldn't say," she replied.

"But you were so good with her this afternoon." Wyatt put his hands on his hips.

"Lucky, that's all. I just…remembered a few things." The same strange look flitted over her features once more.

Wyatt took the coffee to the table. "You fooled me. You looked like you knew exactly what you were doing." So much so that Wyatt had felt completely inept. A feeling he despised. He was used to being the one in control.

Elli and Darcy walked the length of the kitchen and back. After a few moments, she admitted, "I haven't really cared for a baby before. The things I thought of were simply things I'd heard about. Not from experience, Mr. Black."

Her chin jutted up, closing the subject but making him

want to ask the questions now pulsing through his mind. But then he remembered the old saying—*Don't look a gift horse in the mouth*. He'd benefit from whatever insight she had and be glad of it.

"I don't really know what babies need," he said. "I fed her, patted her back like you did, walked her to sleep, but every time I put her down…"

Wyatt almost groaned. Of course. He'd forgotten one important thing. He'd been so focused on getting the formula the right temperature that he'd forgotten to check her diaper. Not that he had any clue what to do there either.

Pulling calves and shoveling out stalls was far less intimidating than one tiny newborn.

"She's probably due for a diaper change, isn't she." He tried to sound nonchalant. This was a perfect opportunity. Elli must know how to change a diaper. He could simply watch her so he'd know better for the next time.

Instead, Elli came around the corner of the counter and placed Darcy back in his arms. "Here you go, Uncle Wyatt," she said lightly. "You get diaper duty. I'll fix the coffee. Cream and sugar?"

Oh boy, Wyatt thought, looking down into Darcy's pursed face, his smug plan blown to smithereens. He was in for it now.

Will sparks fly between Elli and Wyatt?

Find out in
PROUD RANCHER, PRECIOUS BUNDLE

Available February 2011 from Harlequin Romance

Try these Healthy and Delicious Spring Rolls!

INGREDIENTS

2 packages rice-paper
spring roll wrappers
(20 wrappers)

1 cup grated carrot

¼ cup bean sprouts

1 cucumber, julienned

1 red bell pepper, without
stem and seeds, julienned

4 green onions
finely chopped—
use only the green part

DIRECTIONS

1. Soak one rice-paper wrapper
   in a large bowl of hot water
   until softened.

2. Place a pinch each of carrots,
   sprouts, cucumber, bell
   pepper and green onion on the
   wrapper toward the bottom
   third of the rice paper.

3. Fold ends in and roll tightly
   to enclose filling.

4. Repeat with remaining
   wrappers. Chill before
   serving.

Find this and many more delectable recipes
including the perfect dipping sauce in

NTRSERIESJAN